C.   WW

MW01482532

GUN FURY

GUN FURY

Steven C. Lawrence

Chivers Press ● G.K. Hall & Co.
Bath, Avon, England Thorndike, Maine USA

This Large Print edition is published by Chivers Press, England and by G.K. Hall & Co., USA.

Published in 1996 in the U.K. by arrangement with Lawrence A. Murphy.

Published in 1996 in the U.S. by arrangement with Lawrence A. Murphy.

U.K. Hardcover ISBN 0–7451–3883–7 (Chivers Large Print)
U.S. Softcover   ISBN 0–7838–1538–7 (Nightingale Collection Edition)

The text of this Large Print edition is unabridged.
Other aspects of the book may vary from the original edition.

Set in 16 pt. New Times Roman.

Printed in Great Britain on acid-free paper.

British Library Cataloguing in Publication Data available

Library of Congress Cataloging-in-Publication Data

Lawrence, Steven C.
  Gun fury / Steven C. Lawrence.
    p. cm.
  ISBN 0–7838–1538–7 (lg. print : lsc)
  1. Large type books. I. Title.
PS3562.A916G83   1996
813′.54—dc20
                                          95–38624

CHAPTER ONE

It was one minute before five. Ben McKee lowered his eyes from the wall clock and stepped around the boot-and-shoe counter of his general store. He glanced contentedly, satisfied, about the long wide room as he walked down the center aisle past shelves and counters that bulged with fresh bolts of dry goods, bright prints and percales and calicoes, pants and shirts, underwear, bandannas, the hardware and gun rack, all the products which spoke of a thriving business.

Hiram Loomis, a short bald man of sixty who clerked for Ben, was busy at the candy counter near the front window. He and McKee had been doing exactly what the other merchants of Buffalo Hole had done this Friday. They'd restocked each item on hand, marked the price tags, and arranged the displays to catch everyone's eye during tomorrow's celebration. Loomis pulled his head out of the glass case when the tall storekeeper stopped at the door to look outside. A faint, sweet odor of peppermint-stick followed the clerk to Ben's side. Loomis wiped the sugared stickiness from his hands on the white apron tied about the round bulge of his belly. He glanced through the window, then grinned up at McKee.

1

'Right on time, Ben,' he said.'Who's drivin' today?'

'Freddy.' He smiled. 'I'll bet that caused a howl.'

McKee stepped onto the porch and waited for the buggy that held his family to pull up at the hitchrail.

Charlotte sat quiet and calm holding the tearful Maryann on her lap. The boys, crowded together next to their mother on the driver's side, waved at their father. Seven-year-old Tom had darker black hair than his older brother, and his face was a little fatter, but it was evident that at maturity they'd both be like McKee, perpetually lean tall men of incurable physical energy and rope-like toughness. As usual, Ben had a momentary feeling of thanks that the baby had the same chubbiness, light coloring and fine blonde hair of her mother. It would have been a tragedy if at twenty-three months she showed any tendency toward the string-bean side of the family.

The buggy stopped beyond the red-and-white striped awning, and the boys piled down to the walk. They began to race inside.

'I get a chocolate bar, Dad,' Freddy announced. He elbowed his brother back away from the store doorway.

'Hey. After you tie up,' said McKee.

Freddy halted, turned and reached for the reins. Tom went past his father. 'Hi, Pop! Hi, Mr Loomis! I've got a nickle of my own, Mr

2

Loomis!' Laughing, the clerk followed him inside.

McKee raised both arms to take Maryann. The baby whimpered, clutched at her mother's arm.

Charlotte gave a patient shake of her head. 'Your pride and joy wanted to drive,' she said. 'Just let her hold the reins, Daddy.'

'Here, Freddy. I'll tie her,' said McKee.

The boy had the leather half turned around the rail from which the bark had been peeled by thousands of such tetherings. At nine Freddy already showed a bit of independence, but he kept it in when he dealt with his father.

'Aw, you always give her her way,' he complained as he held the reins out. 'You'd never give in to me and Tommy that way.'

'You want that chocolate?' McKee turned to the seat and placed the thin leather strip between Maryann's tiny hands.

'Gidd'up, Pony. Gidd'up … giddyup,' the child said. The bay mare didn't move, as if she understood this ritual which took place whenever it was Maryann's turn to sit in her mother's lap and drive on these weekly trips to the store. Actually the animal's name was Queen, but after Maryann started to walk, the baby had taken a possessive attitude toward the horse. Maryann had her own private name, her own private way of talking to the mare in the barn behind their house. As far as Maryann was concerned, Pony was one of the family.

3

Ben McKee smiled up at his wife and she smiled at him.

'Hy has everything boxed near the door,' he said.

'There are two or three more things I need.' She picked the reins from the baby's fingers, added firmly, 'That's enough for now, sweetheart. Up now. Daddy'll hold you.'

McKee took his daughter. He held her against his left shoulder and chest while he steadied Charlotte as she stepped off the foot plate. Even though Charl had said the list she'd given him that morning contained everything she needed, he knew she'd have an extra list. Hy would expect one, too. He lowered the baby to the walk. Charlotte gripped the child's hand and started up the steps.

'You round the kids up,' McKee told her. 'I'll put the boxes into the back seat.'

'I should go over to Mae Ward's,' she said, turning her face toward the west end of the business district. 'I told her I'd come in for a fitting weeks ago.'

'Why?' He winked, flicked his eyes from the hem of her dress to her face. 'Let Mae build onto those middle-aged women who need it. You look good to me and that's for sure, lady.'

'Ben . . .' Charlotte said. She glanced around to see if anyone had noticed his slightly rakish stare, or had heard. 'Come on, Maryann, if your father's going to act like that.'

McKee grinned to himself while his wife and

4

daughter moved onto the porch. Charlotte did indeed look good to him, as did his entire family. He gazed at the false-fronted buildings that lined both sides of Main Street, squinting against the August sun, hard and bright on the white dust. He was a lucky man to have such a wonderful marriage and family. Everybody was healthy; Maryann hadn't had any of her croup since early Spring. Last winter had been colder and with more snow than they'd known in the ten years they'd been here in Buffalo Hole. But you couldn't tell about these high-country Colorado winters. Next winter could be mild...

He whipped a halter knot around the rail, thinking again how lucky he had been to find Charlotte in a town like Amarillo. She had made such a major change in his life—from lawman to storekeeper. Now it seemed he'd never even worn a gun, leastwise lived by using one. They'd had their own home at the east edge of town for six years, with a barn and a large yard for the children. The house was all paid for; the store increased its business each year. He didn't owe any bills. He wasn't a rich man, not rich in terms of ranchers like Will Oursler and Oakley Haycox who owned the two biggest spreads in the Hole. But McKee had never wanted to be wealthy like that. He'd come here for a different kind of security. This valley with only one pass coming into it, had offered the exact type of safety he'd wanted.

Snow closed in the Hole from November to late May each year. That and the security of good, close friends was what McKee had looked for and found.

Inside the store Hy Loomis was busy at the dry-goods counter cutting a length of cloth for Charlotte. Maryann, for the moment, waited still and quiet beside them. Freddy chewed on his candy bar while he handled the harness display. During the past six months he'd become interested in horses, and any new rig that came into the store had to be inspected by him the minute he spotted it. Tom was in his own private cowboy-and-Indian world near the gun rack. He'd been forbidden to touch the weapons. He simply stood and studied the line of handguns, carbines and shotguns which were always locked behind a barred glass case.

McKee had put two boxes filled with groceries and supplies in the rear of the buggy when Freddy followed him out onto the porch. The boy carried a snaffle bit in his right hand. He held it up for his father to see.

'How about a new one of these for Queen, Dad?' he asked. 'The bit she's got now's almost two years old.'

'Sure. If you get the money together.'

'Aw, Dad.'

'Don't "Aw, Dad" me. You took over the care of Queen on your own hook. And you've done a good job. You agreed you'd buy the small things she'd need out of what I pay you.

Candy bars before supper must be more important to you, or you'd've saved your money for that bit.'

He pushed the screen door open. Freddy followed him in silence. Tom had come down the aisle from the guns. He had two boxes of caps in his hand.

'Hey, look what I got, Freddy,' he said joyfully. 'Both boxes for a nickle. I got them in the sale.'

'Sale?' McKee said. He glanced at where old Loomis was rolling Charlotte's cloth. He'd have to speak to Hy about these sudden sales that went on when the kids came in on Fridays. McKee pointed to the last box which waited transportation outside. 'You two get on that and put it into the buggy.'

He took the bit from Freddy and walked to the dry-goods counter. Maryann saw him approach. She let out a happy squeal and ran to him. He picked her up and held her close and kissed her smooth pudgy cheek.

'Anything else on that extra list?' he said to Charlotte.

She didn't look around or answer, but Loomis gave McKee a knowing grin. In that moment, when he'd glanced up, the bald clerk noticed the three men who'd come into the store. McKee didn't see them. He waited for the usual remark Charlotte gave when he joked with her about her extra lists. 'If you were a woman running a house, you'd understand

7

how things pop up.' He waited, watching her. She was thirty-two this last spring, seven years younger than himself, yet she looked closer to twenty. Her dark blue dress set off her light coloring and hair. Her eyes were soft gray and quiet and deep. Her nose, which she despised, was thin and faintly bobbed. He'd liked it from the first moment he'd seen her.

'Customers, Ben,' said Loomis, nodding toward the front of the store.

'You handle them,' McKee told him. Hy went down the aisle. McKee picked up the cloth. 'Anything else, lady?'

'No. I think we'll go right home. I want to make some pies for the box luncheon tomorrow.'

'What about Mae Ward's?'

She smiled, twisted her figure slightly. 'My husband likes me just as I am, sir.'

Grinning, he walked along the aisle with her. Hy Loomis met them before they reached the front door.

'These men want you to wait on them, Ben,' the clerk said. 'One of them's huntin' for some special kind of belt.'

McKee stared across the wide room. The three waited beneath the overhead lamp near the cracker barrel. They all wore expensive-looking dark suits, and his first impression was that here was money and power. The feeling had nothing to do with their clothing. It was in the way the men stood, in the casual, serious

8

way they watched him.

McKee said, 'Hy, you get Charl and the kids going. After, go over to the post office and see if the papers came in on the stage.' He held Maryann out for Charlotte to take.

'You'll be home early, won't you, Ben,' she said. 'The boys want to help you clean the buggy. And Freddy wants Billy Royce to come with us tomorrow.'

'I don't know about Billy. That'd be up to his folks.'

'Ben, his mother's been too sick to go anywhere since she had the baby. Billy is Freddy's best friend.'

'You ask his mother then. Tell her we'd be glad to take him if she doesn't need him around the house.'

'I will, Ben.' She started out.

McKee turned, then walked back up the center aisle. One of the men stepped out in front of the others. He was tall, only an inch or so shorter than McKee. He was perhaps sixty, with the lean, disciplined body of a professional soldier under his tailored black broadcloth. He wore black patent leather shoes and an expensive black Stetson.

'That your family, storekeeper?' he asked when McKee reached him.

McKee nodded, not liking the question, or the tone in which it was asked. There was nothing to be learned from the man's features, which were tanned and leather hard, nor from

9

his eyes which were merely sharp dark globes beneath heavy gray eyebrows. His hair was as silvery-gray. He was dressed like a banker or a money-rancher, but he was not simply another banker or rancher, McKee knew. He was too cold, too controlled. Something about him was familiar to McKee, something in his blunt, taut speech and stance that hinted at an explosive power within the man. But McKee couldn't quite place him.

'My clerk said you asked for a special kind of belt,' McKee reminded him.

The man nodded. 'A money belt. I carry a lot of cash around with me.'

McKee shook his head. 'I'm sorry, we don't carry them.' He pointed toward the west end of town. 'We have a hostler at the livery who's a wonder with leather. Maybe he...'

'You don't recognize me, Deputy?' the man said, smiling briefly at McKee.

The words brought an ominous silence. The other two men didn't move. The taller, dressed in a gray broadcloth, was soft and loosely built. A thick brown beard and reddish hair hid most of his calm, apple-cheeked face. He applied himself to a week-old edition of the Denver Post on the grocery counter. He frowned now, intent on the front page, apparently immune to everything except his immediate preoccupation. The shorter, also wearing black broadcloth, was a barrel-chested, blocky man with huge shoulders and a wide forward-

10

thrust head of coarse black hair. He studied McKee like a wary watchdog.

'No,' McKee answered. 'I can't say I remember you.'

'It was in Don Pedro, eighteen years ago … in eighty-two,' the tall man said. 'You stopped a bank robbery with Jim Hutchins. Hutchins was sheriff, and you were his deputy. You killed two boys. The Basso brothers. You and Hutchins. You got their father and had him sent up for twenty years. Only he got out five years early for good behavior.'

McKee knew the man now. Giles Basso. Eighteen years older, gray-haired … He remembered the day they'd gotten the Bassos in the plaza of Don Pedro. He never had figured out why they'd hit the small bank in the New Mexico town. Less than a thousand dollars had been in the safe. Basso and his sons had run out to cross the wide-open plaza, nothing more than a half-acre of sunbaked sand. The banker's yells had brought McKee and Hutchins running from the adobe jail. The Bassos didn't even reach the ancient adobe church at the eastern limit of the town. Basso started to shoot, then his sons. His two sons died beside the crumbling red walls of a deserted building. Basso, with a bullet through his hip, was taken as he'd tried to crawl under some gourd vines and a patch of sunflowers which grew at the rear of the church.

McKee remembered how Basso had looked

11

in court. He had been heavier then, like a sullen, vicious animal. He'd stared across the small courtroom at McKee and Hutchins as if his one thought was to kill them both. He'd threatened to do just that after he'd been sentenced. The hate was still in his eyes the day McKee and Hutchins left him at the Albuquerque prison. Today McKee felt that hate; it was just as vicious and dangerous as it had been. But it wasn't in Basso's face. Basso studied him with a businesslike stare, his eyes frowning and black, his dark features set in a closed, unrevealing expression.

'You got out three years ago,' McKee said quietly. 'I'd say you've done well since then.'

'Very well. I've built up a cattle-buying business. A nice safe business. I buy all the stock a valley like this will sell, and I market it for the ranchers. It's a very lucrative business.'

'I'm surprised you haven't come here before this.'

Basso smiled slightly, but it didn't relieve the expression about his eyes. 'It took me three years to learn where you'd gone.' He glanced around at his men. 'We went back to Don Pedro. Did you know that Hutchins died seven years ago? He's buried behind the church.'

'Yes, I heard.'

The deep-set eyes hardened. 'I wanted to see him,' Basso said tightly. 'I wanted to see him about my two boys he cut down. But I've found you now. And you've got a family, too.'

12

McKee said, 'Look, Basso. I haven't had on a gun in ten years, but if you start trouble...'

'Trouble?' Basso interrupted. 'Who said anything about trouble?' He undid a front button, then pulled open his coat to show he did not carry a gun. He motioned to the other two men. 'Jonas Foss and Cooley are both fast with guns, lightning fast, Deputy. Or should I say "Sheriff"? I heard you made an even bigger name as sheriff while I was away.' He spoke directly to the taller of the two. 'Show him, Cooley.'

Both men opened their coats and showed gunless hips.

'They're the two fastest draws I could find,' Basso said. 'As fast as you were. They've got permission to wear guns in this town. I carry a great deal of cash on me, and they're my bodyguards. But today I'm not having them wear guns.' He stopped talking, glanced through the front window at the black surrey which had come to a stop beyond the porch. Quickly his eyes returned to McKee. 'I'm going to get you, McKee, the same way you got my family. Only I'm going to do it slow, McKee. Slow, so you'll die five times.'

Loud bootclicks sounded on the porch. The screen door swished inward. Oakley Haycox came up the aisle, a wide smile on his thin face. Haycox owned the second largest ranch in the basin. He was on the Town Council and acted as chairman of the Stockman's Association.

13

He was in his late sixties, but he still had the bone-hard body of a working cowman. He limped a little from a knee which had been broken thirty years ago by a Comanche arrow when he'd been among the first to push cattle out of the Texas Brazos onto the Llano Estacado. That pioneering spirit had brought him into this valley during the early eighties. He and men like Will Oursler had made Buffalo Hole, and he'd naturally be the man for a cattle buyer to contact for business.

'Mr Basso, I've got my surrey out there,' Haycox said. 'We can go out and talk to Oursler now.'

'Fine. Fine, Mr Haycox. I just want a minute to buy some spurs before I go.' He stepped along the boot-and-shoe counter.

Haycox looked at McKee. 'Did Mr Basso tell you why he's here, Ben? He's goin' to buy our stock every year. Every last head we can supply. Hear that, Ben? We won't have to drive our cattle out and compete in the market from now on.'

'He told me, Oakley. It's a wonderful thing.'

'Wonderful! You're damn well right it is. I'll spread the word when I handle the auction at that shindig tomorrow, so the whole county will know.'

Basso was back. He placed a pair of silver spurs on the grocery counter. 'I'll take these.' He drew a fat roll of greenbacks from his pocket, dropped a five-dollar bill beside the

14

spurs. 'Don't bother with the change. I'll be in again for more things. Just keep a record.'

'Those spurs won't fit you,' McKee told him. 'They're too small.'

'Well, I'll try them on in the surrey. If they're too small, I'll bring them back.' He started for the door.

McKee took a step after him. 'Look, they're children's spurs. They're too small. Let me...'

'Don't keep us here,' Haycox said, a bit irritated with McKee's insistence. 'I'll need all the time I can get to talk Oursler into coming into town. If the spurs don't fit, we'll drop them off at your house.'

'That's right,' Basso said, nodding. 'I'll leave them at your house, storekeeper.'

He left McKee standing alone and went out with Haycox, followed by his two men.

Ben McKee took a step after them, but then he stopped. There was no way he could hold Basso in here, no way he could do anything to the man. He moved to the window and watched Basso and Haycox ride east along Main in the surrey. The other two men had remained behind. One crossed the street to the hotel. The taller walked slowly, leisurely, down toward the east end of town.

McKee opened the screen door and looked up Main. Two blocks west, Hy Loomis was talking to a man on the boardwalk in front of the bank. McKee stepped to the edge of the porch and waved. The clerk saw him. Loomis

15

headed back to the store.

McKee went inside. He took the coat of his blue, lightweight serge from its hook beside the storeroom door. He put the coat on and waited for the clerk to come in. He tried to stay calm, to act natural, but he could not hold down the hard little fist of fear that had solidly gripped his heart.

CHAPTER TWO

Hy Loomis pushed the screen door open and came inside.

'I'm going home for a while, Hy,' McKee told the clerk. 'If I shouldn't get back, you lock up.'

'Sure, Ben.' His round face studied McKee's. 'What's wrong, Ben?'

'Nothing. Nothing serious.' He turned, then walked into and through the back storeroom. He kept everything he didn't have on display in here, extra bolts of cloth, every conceivable item of clothing, tinned and boxed food. In the center of the room a half-dozen, well-cured hams hung from hooks. Many of the valley homesteaders lacked money until they built up their farms or ranches. McKee allowed them purchases as they needed, and he took their products in trade. His cash balance was never high, but he always had plenty of eggs, bacon,

16

jellies, jams, comforters, chickens and hams on hand for barter. He stepped out into the daylight and closed the door behind him.

There was a little wind. Far to the north slight traces of dark cloud had started to build up around Elbert Peak. The sky was a solid brassy blue above the hot land. McKee, who seldom noticed the heat, felt a sticky sweat across his back while he cut through the yards toward his home. He didn't know quite what to expect from Basso. The man certainly wouldn't make trouble with Haycox in the surrey with him. But the tall man who'd been with Basso had headed in this direction. That could mean anything.

He circled a shallow hole which had been started for a cesspool behind the Uris house two blocks from his own. He and Charlotte had rented three rooms in the rear of the hotel until they'd saved enough money to build their home. Charlotte had drawn the plans from a two-floor eastern Cape she'd seen in Harper's Magazine, kitchen and pantry and living room and parlor down, with three bedrooms upstairs. It had looked a bit strange at first, all alone in a grove of cottonwoods three hundred yards from the business district. As Buffalo had grown, more houses were built out from the edge of town. Now the McKee home appeared to strangers who visited the Hole as simply another neat residence in a steadily growing community.

17

The small barn at the rear of the house had gone up two years ago when they'd bought Queen and the buggy. This building, its cleanliness and maintenance, had been Freddy's responsibility from the beginning. McKee wasn't surprised to find his older son inside rubbing down the mare when he stepped through the back doorway.

Freddy glanced over his shoulder at the click of the latch. He watched silently while his father secured the inside lock. The horse, an endless eater, caught sight of McKee. It switched its tail, but didn't interrupt its munching of oats. Freddy came out of the stall. He held a worn snaffle bit in his hand. He'd apparently kept it close by him until his father came home.

'Hi, Dad. See this,' he said, displaying the frayed bit. 'Queen really needs that new one. How about payin' me two weeks ahead for takin' care of her. And I'll get the new one.'

'I'll talk about that later. Where's your brother?'

'In the yard. Mom said to stay close 'cause we're eatin' soon.'

'You stay in here until I call you,' McKee told him. 'I don't want either of you leaving the yard.'

'Okay, Dad. What about the bit, Dad?'

'All right, I'll settle it with you tomorrow.'

He heard his son's, 'Oh, boy!' behind him as he moved out into the daylight. The low, sharp

18

clap-clap of caps came to him from the right side of the house. He called, 'Tom . . . Tommy.'

The black-haired seven-year-old appeared from around the back corner of the house. A wide grin was on his small face. He jammed his toy revolver into the holster he wore, and asked, 'Watch my draw, Pop. Watch.'

His right hand reached down. It came up with the cap-pistol snapping. 'That how you did it, Pop? That how you did it when you were sheriff?'

'You're faster than I was, Tom. You stay in the yard. I don't want either you or Freddy to leave the yard.'

'Sure, Pop. Mom says we're havin' supper right now. She's makin' pies. Apple pies.'

'Good. Stay here now.'

McKee went up the back steps. He opened the kitchen door.

Charlotte looked out from the pantry. She'd unpacked the supplies she'd brought from the store. Tinned goods, boxes and bags waited on the table and sinkboard to be put in their proper places. She came halfway across the room, met him and kissed him. 'I didn't think you'd be home so soon,' she said. 'I haven't even started supper yet.'

He stared down at the empty playpen. 'Where's Maryann?'

'Dreaming in her crib. She fell asleep on the ride home.' She took a box of crackers off the table, held it in her hand while she studied him.

19

He glanced into the front living room. 'Anyone stop here?' he asked.

'Yes. A man left a pair of spurs a few minutes ago. He said he was going out to bring Will Oursler into town.' She smiled. 'That'll be some accomplishment, getting Oursler into town.'

He walked into the living room. The silver spurs lay on the small oak table beside his leather chair. He moved past the walnut sideboard and the overstuffed couch to the windows. He inched the white curtain aside and stared out, first gazing up Main, then eastward and again toward the business district.

Charlotte watched him from the kitchen doorway. 'What's wrong?' Her voice was calm, the patient wife who has work of her own to do. 'If it's that man, he left town in Oakley Haycox's surrey.'

McKee dropped the curtain into place. He'd seen no sign of Basso's man. The street on either side of the house was empty.

'What did he say?' McKee asked.

'Just that he'd bought those spurs in the store and they were too small. He was very nice about it, Ben.'

'There's nothing very nice about that man, Charl. Do you remember I told you about the first shootout I took part in? The one in New Mexico?'

'Yes.'

'That man was the father of the two we had to kill.'

'And he's come here,' she said in an entirely different voice. 'For you?'

'Now don't get nervous, dear. Don't let this get you.'

Charlotte shook her head, slowly. 'He was so quiet. He spoke so calmly. He laughed about his mistake. He said it was his mistake and if you didn't want to, you wouldn't have to return his money.' A sudden frightened look spread across her face. 'Ben, he said he'd heard we had a son who was interested in horses, and if you wanted you could give the spurs to him.' She paused, then added in a small voice, 'Oh, Ben, this is what we came all the way up here to escape.'

McKee stepped close to her, put both his hands on her shoulders. 'Calm down now. He hasn't done anything.'

'He has, Ben. He's come right into our house. What did he say to you?'

He sighed, patted her shoulders. 'Look, if I thought you'd lose control of yourself, I wouldn't have...'

'What did he say? Tell me.' She pulled away from his hands and stood watching him. She held the crackers tightly against her breast. Her fingers were white where they gripped the box. 'Now, Ben.'

He told her with quiet controlled words exactly what had been said in the store. He

21

tried to hold down the inference of the danger to her and the children, but as he spoke he saw more and more clearly himself the depth of Basso's threat. It was as if his effort at quietness and control somehow increased the terrifying impact of exactly what he was saying.

'Oh, Ben,' she breathed. 'Those two gunmen with him ... and all you did was listen?'

'I couldn't do anything else. They didn't have guns. If they had, I certainly wasn't wearing one. That's the worst part of this whole thing. Basso didn't come here to cause a shootout. This is nineteen hundred, Charl. He realizes the days of gunfights are gone. He's cleverer than...'

'Dad! Hey, Dad! Dad!' Freddy's screams tore in through the window from the yard, killing McKee's words. McKee broke into a run for the kitchen.

'Dad! Dad, make Tom stop! Put it down, Tom!'

McKee threw open the back door. His heart jumped. Freddy stood in the open barn doorway, both arms stretched high above his head. In front of him was his smaller brother. Tom was laughing hilariously and pointing a real twin-barreled derringer at Freddy's chest.

'Put that gun down, Tom!' McKee ordered.

Tommy glanced around, then turned with the weapon still up level. 'Ha, ha, Dad. I scared him. I scared him.'

'Give me that gun!'

Tommy's laughter softened. He held out the derringer. 'I was just tryin' to scare Freddy. I did scare him good.'

McKee took the weapon from his son's fingers. The instant he had it in his hand he slapped Tom's face hard. 'What did I tell you about not pointing guns at people?'

Tears streamed down the boy's cheeks. One small hand covered the red spot where he'd been hit. 'Gee, I wasn't gonna shoot.'

'This is a real gun. You could see that. It's loaded. Where did you get it?'

'That man gave it to me,' the child sobbed. 'He called me 'round the side of the house and gave it to me. He said it wasn't loaded and I should give it to you.'

'What man?'

'A man with a beard. He was tall like you.'

'Red-bearded. In a gray suit?'

'Yuh. Yuh, Pop.' He rubbed one dusty hand at his tears, smearing the dirt across his cheek. 'He said it was a joke on you, Pop. He said it wasn't loaded, and I could give Freddy a good scare with the gun before I brought it in to you.'

'Oh, my Lord. Dear Lord,' Charlotte said softly.

In her upstairs bedroom of the house, Maryann, awakened by the loud yells and talk, had started to cry. Charlotte and the boys stood silently, watching husband and father.

23

Queen kicked once against the stall. The bay mare had interrupted her meal to watch. Her large dark eyes were on McKee, as if as part of the family she also understood the gravity of the situation.

McKee slipped the derringer into his coat pocket. 'Take the kids inside,' he told Charlotte. 'I'm going up to get Nate Royce.'

'All right. I'll lock the doors, Ben.'

'Keep calm.' He patted her arm. 'Nothing's happened yet, dear. You tell the boys the reason for this. I'll get right back.' He looked at his sons. 'Okay, boys, into the house with your mother.'

He didn't move while the children started toward the kitchen door ahead of Charlotte. Before they reached the steps, Tom glanced around at him.

'Pop, I'm sorry. I'm really sorry, Pop.'

'Get inside. I'll talk to you later.'

Tommy whimpered, moved faster. McKee waited until his wife and sons closed the door behind them. Then he walked along the side of the house to the street.

The whiskered, gray-suited man was nowhere in sight. McKee hadn't expected he would be, after what he'd done. He'd no doubt headed straight for the hotel so he'd be well clear of the houses when the shot sounded. Yet McKee couldn't be certain Basso hadn't had his man give the derringer to young Tom in order to draw McKee into the street. If he was

24

shot now, a gun would be found in his pocket. It would look no better for him than it would for the man who killed him. McKee quickened his stride, kept to the center of the road.

The last thing McKee wanted was to cause shooting here along the line of houses. Most of his neighbors were at their evening meals. He could smell frying steak and onions and cabbage, and fresh bread that had just been taken out of an oven. In the yard closest to the business district, two boys and a girl played a final game of Kick-the-Can before being called in to wash their faces and hands and come to supper. Most of these homes and the store buildings at this end of Main were new, less than five or six years old. The jeweler, furniture store, the restaurant, the barbershop with its adjoining billiard parlor, every building including his own store between the residential section and the sheriff's office, had been built since McKee had settled in Buffalo. Five blocks had been added to the original wooden constructions a block long on each side of Main which housed the jail, two saloons and the two-story Buffalo Hotel. No one stood on the hotel porch now, or looked out through the lobby door. The walks and street were still and empty beyond the jail, the houses at the west end of town just as evening quiet as those behind him.

McKee stepped up onto the right-hand boardwalk when he was directly opposite the hotel. Twenty feet ahead the door of the sheriff's office was wide open. McKee breathed in deeply, feeling the coolness of the air. To the north the black clouds that had rolled up around Elbert Peak would soon work out toward the high sandstone cliffs which closed in that side of the Hole. The temperature had dropped as the damp wind blew down off the mountains. McKee shivered. A storm was a bad thing now. The night would be black-dark. Rain and wind would cover a man's movements and sounds.

The sheriff's office was a bare room with patched plaster walls and unpainted pine floorboards. Nate Royce sat with his bootheels on his rolltop desk while he read a book. He glanced up as McKee entered. 'Well, Ben. Glad to see you.' He took one foot off the desk and kicked a cane-backed chair toward McKee. 'How's things at the store?'

'Fine ... fine. Emma feeling any better?'

'No, she's 'bout the same.' He stared up at McKee.

'Nate, I've got some trouble.' McKee drew the derringer from his pocket and laid it on the spur-scarred desktop. 'A man gave my Tommy this as a plaything.'

The sheriff closed the book, lowered his other foot. He sat straight, quiet while he listened to McKee's story. He was a square-faced, black-haired man in his late forties. He'd come to Buffalo Hole nine years ago as deputy,

26

and when the sheriff had died after a heart attack, he'd been elected to the position. He'd married the daughter of one of the local hay farmers. Now he had two children, a baby of six months and a boy of eight who played with Freddy and Tommy McKee. Royce made no movement as he listened. His thick jowls tightened at the end. He nodded to Ben McKee.

'I know them,' he said. 'Oak Haycox came in with them for permits to carry guns. I didn't know 'bout Basso, Ben. I issued the permits.'

'You didn't issue any right for them to give a loaded derringer to a seven-year-old kid.'

Royce nodded. 'We'll go over,' he said solemnly. He stood and jammed the derringer inside the waistband of his trousers. He opened the bottom drawer of the desk, took out a holstered .44 Colt, and buckled the weapon around him.

The hotel lobby, a wide low-ceilinged room with a closed door leading to the Frontier Saloon, smelled slightly of stale beer and tobacco. Placed neatly about the carpetless floor were matched leather chairs and a long leather divan, each sided by a polished brass spittoon. A coal-oil lamp which hung above the registration desk threw shadows across the key rack and brightly polished lithographs on the walls.

McKee followed the sheriff to the desk. Ben had kept his eyes on the hotel windows while

27

they'd crossed from the jail. He hadn't seen any sign that they were watched. No one watched them now in the deserted lobby.

Royce slapped the service bell on the counter. 'Tetterman. Mr Tetterman,' he called.

Somewhere above them a door opened, then closed. The staircase creaked, and a tall, boney man whose balding head and long face gave an impression of propriety came down. He wore a spotless white shirt, dust cuffs on the sleeves. A thick gold watch chain swung from a pocket of his vest.

'What is it, Nate?' the hotel owner said coldly. 'This is a hotel. You know I keep things quiet for my guests.'

'I want to see one of those guests,' said Royce. 'Those three men who came in on this morning's stage. They're stayin' here.'

The hotelman nodded. 'Mr Basso and his two bodyguards. Mr Basso's in twenty-two. The others are in twenty-four.'

'The whiskered one's the man I want.' He motioned to McKee and started for the staircase.

'Wait. Wait a minute, Nate,' said Tetterman. 'I don't want you to break in on my guests. Mr Basso's been very generous...' He saw his words did no good. He hurried after McKee and the lawman, trailed them up the stairs. On the top landing, he gripped Royce's arm. 'What is this, Nate?'

'I want to talk to those bodyguards.' The

sheriff jerked his arm free and walked to the door which had '24' painted on the panel in three-inch white numbers. He knocked.

Muffled footsteps sounded within the room. The door swung in. The husky, barrel-chested man stared out. 'Yeah?' he asked.

Royce said to McKee, 'This the man?'

'No. The other one.'

Royce drew the derringer from his waistband. He pushed the door open wide and stepped into the room.

'Hey, what is this?' the huge man questioned. Tetterman began to move in beside the sheriff, but Royce elbowed the hotel owner aside. Royce held the weapon up so the gray-suited whiskered man who lay sprawled on the bed could see it. 'You,' Royce ordered. 'Come over here.'

The man sat. 'What in hell is this?'

'You gave this gun to a boy a little while ago. Mr McKee here says...'

'Hold on right there,' the man cut in. 'I didn't give that gun or anything to any kid. I've been in this room the past fifteen minutes.'

Tetterman spoke then. 'I'm sorry, Mr Cooley. I couldn't stop them from coming up here.' He turned to Royce. 'He's right, Sheriff. He's been in this room. I just brought something up for these gentlemen to drink.'

'Not fifteen minutes ago,' McKee said, looking at the whiskey bottle and glass on the marble-top dresser. 'This one was at my house.

29

He gave Tommy that loaded derringer.'

'You're crazy,' Cooley answered. His apple-cheeked face behind the reddish beard was as sure and innocent as it had been inside the general store. 'I've been right in here. With you, right, Jonas?'

'I'll damn well swear to that,' the huge man said. 'Listen, Sheriff. I don't know what's goin' on.' He waved one big hand brusquely at McKee. 'We were in this one's store with Mr Basso. He gave us a hard time over Mr Basso bringin' trouble to this town by havin' so much cash with him. He said he was a lawman or somethin'.' He looked at Cooley, who nodded agreement. 'Mr Basso didn't want no trouble, so he gave me his cash to have locked up in the hotel safe. Cooley and me brought the money over here.'

'That's correct,' Tetterman said. 'I've got more than ten thousand dollars in my safe. I put it in with Jonas Foss just fifteen minutes ago.'

'With Foss?' McKee asked. 'What about Cooley?'

'Listen, you,' Cooley said. 'I don't know what you're tryin'. Jonas came in the front. I covered the back. You didn't expect us not to be careful with ten thousand, did you?' He faced directly at Royce. 'You look, Sheriff,' he went on, pulling his coat open for the lawman to see he wore no gun. 'Mr Basso told us that this storekeeper might make trouble. He made

30

us leave our guns off while the money's in the safe. He figures we don't wear guns, we can't be forced into any gunfights.' He glanced at his companion. 'Let him see, Jonas.'

The huge man opened his coat. He didn't carry a weapon. Royce nodded, slowly. He looked at McKee.

'He gave Tommy that gun, Nate,' McKee stated. 'That Basso's exactly what I said he is.'

'This is foolish,' Cooley said. 'I don't know what he's told you, Sheriff, but Mr Basso's owner of the biggest cattle-buyin' business west of these Rockies. You can check on him, Sheriff.'

Again Royce nodded. 'Don't you men leave this room,' he said.

'You've no right to...' Tetterman began, then silenced when the lawman snapped, 'I don't want either of them out of this room. Not until I talk to this Basso.'

Tetterman sputtered. Cooley spoke clearly. 'We won't leave, Sheriff. But you better talk to our boss fast. He's doin' big things for this basin. You better not...'

'I'll talk to him,' Royce said. He opened the door.

McKee followed the lawman into the hallway and downstairs. Once on the porch Royce halted. He slipped the derringer into his pocket. 'I'll hold this,' he remarked.

'Nate, Cooley must've run up behind the houses. That's why I didn't see him on the

31

street. He went in the back door while Tetterman was putting the money in the safe.'

Slowly Royce gave a nod. 'I'll talk to Basso.' He started off the porch.

McKee touched the lawman's arm. 'Nate, Cooley did give my boy that gun.'

Royce's stare was as serious as McKee's. 'What did you expect me to do, lock them both up? With Tetterman for a witness, and both of them telling the same story? You were a lawman. You know what I can do and what I can't do.'

McKee dropped his hand. Royce left him and crossed toward the sheriff's office.

Ben McKee stood at the edge of the porch without moving for a few moments. The sun had started to set in the west. Thick shadows stretched across the width of Main. The clouds to the north completely covered the top of Elbert Peak, and thunder made a distant rumble behind the mountains. He looked at the general store. He'd planned to keep Hy Loomis late tonight until they had the shelves and counters set up exactly as he wanted for tomorrow's rush. Now the store and the promise of a good business day meant nothing to him. His only thought was to get home and take care of his family.

CHAPTER THREE

He kept to the sidewalk while he walked home.
He wasn't sure what Cooley and Jonas would
do until Basso returned. He'd seen enough men
of their type when he'd worn a badge. They
were ruthless, merciless, but they'd hired out to
a strong man who demanded strict obedience
to his orders. Either would call him out into the
center of this street the minute Basso wanted.
The fact that he'd not handled a gun in ten
years would make them even more willing to
do their job that way. But Basso had his own
vicious plan in this. The derringer in a boy's
hand had been the first step. The next might
not be taken until Basso got back.

McKee shivered at the thought of what
could have happened to Freddy if Tom had
squeezed the trigger. He'd seen plenty of bullet
wounds. He'd patched up many men, but he'd
helped bury more. Slugs from a derringer did
horrible things if they hit just right. They could
tear a hole through a grown man's chest big
enough to thrust half his fist into. With a boy
the results would have been terrible ... He
drove the picture from his mind. He wet his lips
with his tongue, forced himself to relax. After
all these years of marriage, Charlotte could
read his face. She was a worrier and she'd be
bad enough without seeing how deeply he was

33

affected.

He saw her when he was still three houses from his own. She waited in the front living room window, the curtain pulled open so she could look out and watch for him. She dropped the curtain into place, stepped to the hallway door, and opened it as he came up the steps.

The good smell of baking pies was strong in the house, and he knew she'd made a roaring fire in the range that would keep out the storm's coldness. She would have already opened the ceiling vent to Maryann's room so the air up there wouldn't get damp while the baby slept. It was a precaution they took against croup whenever one of these summer storms struck. The house felt warm and comfortable and safe.

But Charlotte's eyes were very wide and troubled. She backed from the hallway into the living room. 'I didn't see Nate take that man over to the jail,' she said.

'He didn't feel he had to,' he lied. 'Stop looking so scared, honey. It won't do the boys any good. We've got things in motion now. Nate knows what to be watching for if Basso tries anything.'

'What do you mean? Couldn't he see they've already tried to do enough harm to us? He should have arrested the man.'

'Nate couldn't arrest him. He...'

'That man gave our son a terrible weapon. Tom could have killed Freddy. You gave Nate

34

that gun, didn't you? He saw it?'

McKee nodded his head. He'd tried to talk around the whole truth and lessen the fear Charlotte already felt. He'd been wrong to do that. She had a right to be told everything. 'The man denied he gave Tom the gun,' he said. Then he continued on.

Charlotte stood with her back to the wide stone hearth and listened to his account of what had taken place in the hotel. 'He has two witnesses to his story,' he said at the end. 'Tetterman would be enough by himself. There was nothing Nate could do but let him go with only a warning.'

She stood absolutely still. He kissed her forehead. 'We're locked up for the night now, dear. We'll sleep on it and decide what to do tomorrow.'

'Mom,' Freddy's voice called in from the kitchen. 'Maryann's through with her egg. She's tryin' to take my cookies, Mom.'

'Give her one,' Charlotte told him. 'I'll give you some more.'

She stared toward the kitchen door, shook her head. 'Ben, I tried to be calm about this. I did, but all of a sudden I remembered how it was in Amarillo. I couldn't sit in there and eat with the children. I wanted to take them up to their rooms and pull down the shades. I didn't. I tried not to let them see how worried I am.' She looked into his eyes. 'That man Basso knew just which house to come to. He knew

35

little things about our children, like Freddy being a bug on horses. This isn't anything we can sleep on. It's a real threat now. It'll be just as real in the morning.'

'I know, dear.'

Freddy appeared in the kitchen doorway. 'Mom, Maryann's broken the cookie all to pieces. She's throwin' it on the floor.'

'All right. I'll be in. You finish your supper.'

The boy hesitated. 'Dad, what did Mr Royce do?'

'He's going to watch those men,' McKee answered. 'You finish your supper like Mom wants.'

Freddy returned to the table. Charlotte said, 'Tell them everything so they won't be careless. I'll take the baby upstairs.' She started toward the kitchen door, then paused. 'Tom's broken-hearted. Let him make up. He hasn't eaten very much, he's so ashamed.'

McKee followed her into the kitchen and waited while she carried the baby upstairs.

Tom was bent over his half-empty plate. He wouldn't look at his father. Freddy was busy with a mouthful of cookie. Ben stopped at the sink and gazed out through the yard to the open barn door. The black clouds were over the town, making the dusky evening light thin and eerie. Pinkish lightning played across the sky above the sandstone cliffs. Low thunder rumbled in the mountains. McKee turned from the window, studied his sons. He was

36

silent for another minute before he spoke.

'Your mother told you why that man gave Tom the derringer,' he said. Both boys nodded. He watched them, gauging for their depth of understanding. 'Things like this don't happen often,' he added. 'But a lawman, or a man who has been a lawman, has to always watch out for them.'

Freddy asked, 'Why's he after us? We didn't do anything.'

'This Basso wants to hurt me,' McKee explained. 'He blames me for what happened to his sons. He doesn't blame himself. The best way he can hurt me is to harm you. He knows I love you, and that I'd be terribly hurt if anything happened to you.'

Tom's lower lip trembled. The boy bit down. 'Pop, I didn't mean to hurt Freddy,' he said. 'Honest. That's why I didn't even touch the triggers.'

'You pointed the gun at him. That was enough, Tom.' He saw the child was on the edge of tears. 'What you did is over, Tom. You've had your punishment. I want your word you'll never point a gun, any kind of a gun, at another human being.'

'I won't. I promise I won't.' His small face brightened.

'Dad, the one who gave Tommy the gun should be in jail,' said Freddy. 'I heard you tell Mom that Billy Royce's father didn't put him in jail.'

37

'Yuh, they shoulda hung him,' Tom agreed.

McKee shook his head. 'Boys, we know that man gave Tom the derringer. But he's denied it. He has two witnesses who'd swear in court he was at the hotel the whole time.'

'He lied,' Tom blurted. 'He gave me that gun. He told me to scare Freddy. I hate him. I'd hang him if I had him. I'd pull my gun if I was sheriff. I'd shoot him fulla holes and I'd hang him.'

Charlotte came in through the hall doorway. She halted near the table, waited with her sons for their father's answer.

'Tommy, that's exactly what should not happen,' McKee said slowly. 'Not in this country. It did happen ten or twenty years ago, but that was because of the times. We don't shoot or hang a man until he's arrested and tried and proven guilty. If people could, you or Mommy, or me or Freddy could be put in jail if someone lied about us. Sheriff Royce could've arrested that man. Basso would have had him out on bail tonight anyway. What we've got to do is stay close to each other, and close to this house, and make certain nothing else can happen.'

Tommy scowled, thought it over, then nodded.

'That's what we're going to do,' McKee said. 'Both of you'll go up and get ready for bed. Mom and I will play rummy with you until you turn in.'

38

'What 'bout Queen?' Freddy asked. 'I haven't fed her yet. Or cleaned out the buggy for tomorrow.'

'You go with Mom. I'll take care of Queen.' McKee met Charlotte's stare. A hint of dissatisfaction was on her face, yet he knew she wouldn't disagree with him in front of the children. 'I'll be right in, Mom,' he told her. He opened the door, then moved out onto the steps.

He hurried through the darkness. The lightning flashes were closer, the rumble of the thunder loud now that he was outside. The damp wind blowing down off the mountains was sharp with the tangy, pungent odor of washed pine and sage. Inside the barn he lighted the lamp which hung near Queen's stall.

The horse jerked her long neck up and down and snorted at him, complaining about the lack of attention she'd received at meal time. She rubbed her rump against the side of the stall when he started to fork fresh hay into the bin.

'Where do you put it?' he said as she began to feast. No matter how much the animal ate, she stayed as sleek and thin as a racehorse.

Queen opened one eye wide at him and her long tail flapped against the boards. She raised her head with a mouthful of hay gripped in her white teeth. McKee patted her neck.

'Pony, if you could only tell other females

your secret,' he said.

The tail again brushed against the sideboards and Queen went on with her meal. He left the barn, halting long enough to close the door to keep out the storm.

Charlotte was waiting in the kitchen when he stepped through the doorway. She'd started to clear the table, but she put her work aside.

'I don't think you said the right thing to the boys,' she told him. 'Basso is out to kill us all. You talked as if...'

'What did you want me to do, tell them it's all right to commit murder the minute someone threatens you? You want them to have more respect for the law than that.'

Her head shook. 'I'm not interested in any law that protects a man who'd try to murder my son.' She kept her voice low. 'I'm afraid I haven't got the belief and patience in the law that you have. I'd take that rifle of yours to the hotel and shoot the three of those men if I thought I could. I'm not interested in the law. I just want to save my family.'

'Charl, you stopped me from carrying a gun once. Do you want me to strap one on again and go up to that hotel? Cooley and Jonas are unarmed. I could kill them both in their room. I could kill Basso before he walks through the lobby. That would save our family, but what would it do to those two boys?'

She was silent for a long minute. Her fine body was taut. If he went to touch her now, he

40

felt she would draw away from him.

'Oh, Ben, what will we do?'

'We'll go up and play cards with the kids. We'll hear their prayers and then get them into bed.' He spoke with a heartiness he did not feel. 'We won't talk about Basso or his men. We won't mention the derringer. Above all we won't remind Tom of his idea to go out and shoot and hang those men. That kid just might try it.'

He touched her hands then. She smiled. Together they walked into the front hallway and to the second-floor staircase.

They heard the noise of a running horse outside, and the squeak and rolling sound of a fast-moving wagon. McKee stepped to the door window. He inched the curtain aside.

Oakley Haycox's black open surrey was rolling past the house. Haycox, at the reins, stared straight ahead while he drove his team of two matched black geldings hard to beat the storm. A fine rain was in the air, a mist of drizzle that gave a wet shine to the lamplight which beamed down from the windows of the closed houses. The surrey passed through one light patch, and Ben and Charlotte could see Basso on the seat beside Haycox. Basso's faintly illuminated face was turned toward their house, his stare calm and cold, intent on the windows of the upstairs bedrooms.

'Oursler isn't with them,' Charlotte said. 'Maybe the cattle deal is off.'

'I doubt it,' McKee told her. 'Oursler only comes in once a year. It certainly wouldn't be during a storm.' He let the curtain fall into place. 'We'll go up. You get the cards out. I want to change into my other pants.'

He followed Charlotte up the stairs. She went into the boys' room while he stepped into their bedroom. He shut the door behind him, then walked directly past the double iron-posted bed to the closet.

He pushed his winter suit to one end of the closet. A .73 Winchester carbine leaned barrel-down against the deepest corner. He lifted the weapon. The hard wooden stock felt strange in his hands after all these years. He began to check the lever when the bedroom door opened.

Charlotte stepped inside. She closed the door.

'The bullets are under my handkerchiefs in the left top bureau drawer,' she said. She came to him and circled her arms around him. 'Whatever you say is the right way, Ben. I was too nervous downstairs. You're the man, and I want exactly what you want in this.'

He kissed her and then stood holding her close to him. He stared down over her shoulder at the dusty weapon gripped in his left hand. There was dust in the barrel. He'd have to clean and oil the works to get it back into the condition he had always kept his guns. He'd do it just as soon as the boys were asleep.

CHAPTER FOUR

The storm struck while they played cards. The four of them were sitting around the boys' double bed when a close clap of thunder rattled the windows and the rain came down in a deluge, as if a great bucket of water had been upset over the town. Maryann, who'd been half-asleep in her crib, climbed out to run terrified into the boys' room with the rest of her family. She hugged her mother until she lost her fright. From then on she made a nuisance of herself crawling over the pillows and sheet. She disrupted the draw-deck in the center of the bed, picked up the discards, and pestered her brothers. She sat in her father's lap and helped him play his hand. McKee cuddled the baby close to him, happy that no one mentioned Basso or the derringer. He listened to the hard pound of the rain against the roof, and he thanked God for giving him his fine family, and for this comfortable warm home to house them all.

After twenty minutes Charlotte left the game to go downstairs and take the last of her pies from the oven. McKee stayed with the children, not wanting to show them his concern. He watched the hallway and didn't relax until she was in the room again. He knew they couldn't go on like this for any length of time. Basso had made his threat less than three hours before, and he was already more on edge than he'd ever been in his life. Charlotte sat at the very end of the bed. She kept her head tilted a bit, listening, as though she expected something would happen.

Tom was the one who brought them back to the subject. His turn came, but he didn't draw. Instead, he looked at his father. 'The Sioux were the ones who'd know how to handle them,' he stated flatly.

'Who?'

'Them crazy killers. The Sioux'd get 'em and they'd skin 'em piece by piece. They'd take their knives and they'd cut in on them, and they'd start skin...'

'Tommy!' said Charlotte. 'Where did you hear talk like that?'

'Dick Lutz told me. We were speakin' 'bout Indians yesterday, and he told me he read it in a book.'

'I don't want you talking like that. Not ever. Do you hear, Tom?'

'Gee, Mom. I only said that's what should be done to those men who are after us.'

'Quiet,' McKee ordered. He was on his feet, moving toward the hall doorway.

They all heard the banging downstairs. Charlotte reached the door a step behind McKee. The loud noise stopped. The only sound in the room was the heavy spatter of the wind-driven rain against the roof and

44

windows.

'The rifle,' Charlotte whispered. 'I'll get it.' She started past McKee. He blocked the way.

The banging came again, loud quick knocking. McKee said quietly, 'It's the front door. I'll answer it.'

Charlotte was going to speak. Ben's eyes stared into hers, told her not to alarm the children. She backed toward the bed, said, 'Stay here, boys. It's just someone at the front door.'

McKee went down the stairs. He doubted that Basso or one of his men would come here in the open. Too much chance of their being seen from one of the other houses. A lightning flash threw bright, vivid flame against the windows. Thunder boomed a moment later.

More knocks pounded before he reached the hallway.

'Yes. Who is it?' McKee asked.

'Hy, Ben. Open up, Ben.'

McKee turned the key in the lock, then opened the door. Hy Loomis, wearing a seaman's southwester and slicker, stepped inside, stomping his feet and muttering against the storm. He dug into his pocket and drew out a key. He gazed from the dark front room to the darkened kitchen.

'Thought you might be turnin' in early,' he said. 'The way you've got your lights out. I locked up. Nobody come in once they saw the storm was goin' to hit.'

'Thanks, Hy. Let me have your coat.'

The stubby clerk began to take off the slicker. 'Ben,' he said. 'I don't know what's happened...' He stopped his talk and glanced toward the second floor. He pulled the slicker closed over his round stomach.

Charlotte and the boys stood at the top of the stairs. 'Hi, Mr Loomis,' Tom called. 'Boy, you look wet.'

McKee said, 'Hy brought the store key, Charl. You get the kids to bed.'

'Go into the kitchen,' she told them. 'I'll come down and give Hy some coffee and pie.' She turned to usher the boys back into their room.

'Good night, Dad,' Freddy and Tom shouted. 'G'night, Pop. G'night, Mr Loomis.'

'Good night, boys. Good night.'

Loomis took off his slicker and hung it on the hall-tree. He followed McKee into the kitchen. McKee struck a match and lighted the table lamp.

Loomis did not sit. He opened his coat. The walnut handle of McKee's Smith and Wesson .44 jutted from under the clerk's belt. McKee had kept the sixgun in the bottom drawer of the store desk in case an attempt was ever made to hold them up. Loomis drew the revolver and held it out to McKee.

'You better keep this,' Loomis said. 'You're goin' to need it, Ben.'

McKee took the weapon. He was holding it

46

in his hand when Charlotte entered from the hall. She did not speak. She stared at the revolver, then into her husband's face.

'I brought that gun from the store,' Loomis told her. 'I stopped in at the Frontier after I closed up. Figured I'd have a drink while I waited for the storm to end. Tetterman was in there talkin' about some trouble Ben had in the hotel.' He hesitated, watched Charlotte to judge if she was aware of the trouble.

Nodding, Charlotte said, 'I doubt that Mr Tetterman told it as it actually happened. Anything affecting his business in the hotel has just one way of appearing to that man.'

'That's right,' McKee said. 'I'll keep the gun, Hy. But we don't want you to get mixed up in this.'

'I am in it. The two you had trouble with were in the saloon, too. They followed me out onto the porch and got me against the wall. They said they were goin' to kill Charlotte and the kids, and you, Ben. Last of all you.'

He looked directly at Charlotte. 'I don't want to scare you, Charlotte, but they meant it. I would've got Nate Royce only he's up with Haycox playin' cards with the cattle buyer. I figured the best thing I could do was get Ben's gun and give it to him.'

McKee nodded. 'Thanks, Hy.' He glanced at Charlotte. She looked haggard and gray. 'You go ahead, Hy. I'll be in early in the morning. I'll see Nate Royce again then.'

Charlotte said, 'Royce ... he showed you how he stands in this. He's playing cards with Basso. That's not helping us.'

'Charl, please,' McKee said. 'We don't know what Nate has in mind. He could be up there...'

'Dad! Hey, Pop!' Both Freddy and Tom yelled through the ceiling grating. 'Dad, we heard noises out in the yard!'

'You kids should be in bed.'

'We heard noises, Dad! Listen! Please, Pop!'

McKee stepped close to the door, listened. The only sound which broke the silence of the kitchen was the rain beating against the house. Thunder rumbled to the south of town as the storm moved out of the valley. McKee unlocked and opened the door a few inches.

The steady rain was the only sound outside. McKee closed the door.

'That was just the rain,' he told the boys. 'Go back to bed.'

'But, Pop, we heard noises.'

'Get back into bed or I'll come up with the strap.' McKee lowered his voice. 'They'll hear noises all night, Charl. See if you can quiet them down.'

Charlotte went into the hallway. Hy Loomis waited until he could hear her footsteps on the stairs before he spoke.

'I didn't mean to frighten her. But those men meant what they said. They acted like they didn't know who I was in the Frontier. Once

48

they got me outside, they knew me all right. They said they'd kill every one of you, and they'd do it slow. I know Charlotte hasn't ever faced anything like this, but I had to come in and tell you.'

'You did right.' McKee gazed toward the front hall. He shook his head. 'Charl has faced something like this before. She knows exactly what it means.'

Loomis' fat face tightened. 'This bad?'

'At the time, yes.' He glanced at the hallway again, returned his eyes to Loomis. 'I was sheriff in Amarillo when we were married. Charl wanted me to quit, but I needed money to start a business. We talked it over and decided I'd stay on for another year, until I had enough money. Things went fine for ten months. The town was getting quiet. We were even thinking we'd stay there. People knew us. They liked us. Charl was carrying Freddy by then.'

He paused. One hand touched the handle of the Smith and Wesson on the table. 'You know how Saturday nights are in a cowtown. This crew came in from one of the local ranches. One of them got drunk and I had to knock him out. He threatened me while I had him locked up. I'd never paid attention to threats. I didn't to him.

'His foreman bailed him out that Sunday. Instead of leaving town that cowhand got hold of a bottle and got mad-drunk. He waited until

49

I was with Charl before he tackled me. We were going to church when he yelled from across the street. He had his gun half out. All I could do was shove Charl out of the way. I took a slug in the thigh before I killed him. Charl landed hard on the street. She almost lost Freddy. For two days we didn't know. I got to thinking about all the threats I'd had since I started wearing a badge. I quit that night. As soon as Charl was better we left.'

'I can see why, Ben.'

'I remembered this town from a trip I'd taken. We believed it was far enough from Texas so I wouldn't have to change my name. A man wants his sons to have his own name. He...' The sound of Charlotte's footsteps on the staircase made him stop. He turned to the hallway.

Charlotte hurried into the kitchen. 'Ben,' she said. 'Someone is out there. I heard the noises from the boys' room.' Freddy and Tom appeared a few steps behind their mother. 'We told you,' Tom added. 'I opened our window. We did hear it.'

McKee picked up the revolver. 'Keep the kids in here, Charl.' He stepped toward the door. 'Hy, kill that lamp.'

Loomis blew the flame out and the room darkened. McKee turned the knob and opened the door slowly. The night was pitch black, the rain was still coming down hard. Low thunder rolled far to the south. Nothing could be heard

50

close by except the rain.

Then loud noises sounded in the barn, the snorts of a horse, something banged hard against wood.

'Stay in here, Hy,' McKee said. He crouched, moved onto the steps. Loomis shut the door behind him.

The noises died inside the barn. They started again, loudly, confusedly, while McKee ran through the ankle-deep mud of the yard. Cold rain drenched his face and clothes. He slid in next to the closed right-hand door and listened.

Queen made the commotion, but he couldn't be sure whether it was a result of the storm, or if someone waited for him to come inside. He crouched lower and, holding the .44 ready, pushed the left door open.

Queen was down in her stall, lying on her left side. She was rolling, almost writhing in an attempt to push herself up onto her front hoofs. She didn't make it. She fell back onto her side, snorting painfully.

McKee, still bent low, moved up the aisle between the stalls. No one was inside, yet someone had been. Wet mud outlined a footprint in the hay near Queen's stall. Close to the horse were more small blobs of mud that had dropped from a boot.

Queen raised her long sleek neck when she heard McKee's approach. She tried to get up again, but succeeded only in kicking the stallboards with one front hoof. Her back right

51

leg was broken, the lower bone from joint to hoof twisted at an odd angle. The animal's wide black eyes stared pleadingly up at McKee.

Footsteps squelched in the mud of the yard, and Loomis ran into the barn. He halted beside McKee. 'Oh, what a terrible thing,' the clerk muttered. 'She must've kicked the stall durin' the storm.'

'That leg was broken by a club,' McKee said. 'See where she's cut. There's no blood on the stall.' He pointed at the mud. 'This was here when I got in.' He looked down at the horse. 'Dammit all to hell ... get Ramon from the livery.'

'Sure...' Loomis turned toward the house.

McKee said, 'Hy, don't tell the kids how it happened. Or how bad it is.'

Loomis nodded and continued on through the yard. McKee knelt beside the horse. His eyes were wet, stinging. Queen began another try at standing. McKee pushed gently against her neck. 'Easy, Pony. Lie quiet. Easy now.'

The horse rested her head on the dirt floor. She lay like a sick child, both eyes concentrated on McKee. He patted her neck, spoke softly to her. She was a wonderful horse, so careful with the children, so easy to handle Freddy could care for her alone when he was just seven. She was the McKees' only transportation, and her leg had been broken for that.

McKee stood. The horse lifted her neck.

52

'No, lay there. Quiet, Pony. Quiet', he said. She lowered her head and lay still. He backed from the stall.

The rear door lock hadn't been touched. There was no trace of mud between the stall and that door. Whoever had attacked the animal had entered by the front. McKee walked to the high double doors.

The storm was over except for a light drizzle. Jagged reddish-white flashes cut the sky above the southern peaks. The thunder that followed the lightning was a low grumble in the damp black night. Freddy and Tom stared out through the kitchen window, their noses pressed flat against the glass. McKee sighed, watching his sons. They'd have to be told about Queen. But he didn't want to tell them before he was positive.

Ramon Lerrazza confirmed what McKee had feared. The Mexican had built the livery eight years ago. He and McKee had been good friends through association at the store and in town functions. He was a slender, straight-backed man with light-brown skin, white teeth and black wavy hair. He was very fair in business and a good family man, which made him popular among the townspeople. His second great love was horses. A deep sadness showed on his shadowed face as he examined the broken leg.

'This was done with maybe an iron bar,' he said to McKee. 'See. Hit here and dug into

53

the bone.'

'Any chance of saving her?'

'No.' One of Queen's wide eyes focused on the hostler. Lerrazza rubbed her neck slowly. 'She is in great pain.' He shook his head. 'I do not understand why anyone would hurt an animal so. And she cannot understand.' He stood. 'I will handle it. And the disposal, if you want.'

'You can't wait 'til the kids are asleep?'

'She's suffered enough. I think now. I will wrap the gun so the shot will muffle. They will not hear.'

McKee nodded. 'All right. Thanks, Ramon.' He looked down at the prostrate horse, then walked to the high front doors. Loomis closed one while he shut the other. The low shot cracked almost immediately inside the barn.

McKee watched the kitchen window. The shadowy forms of his family didn't show any sudden movement. They hadn't heard. When he did tell the boys, it would have a demoralizing affect on them. It would be exactly what Basso wanted. He'd drag his threat out more now, the worst thing for them that could happen. They were locked in the Hole and would be easy to watch. They could only anticipate, fear what would come. McKee couldn't let his family live like that...

He drew the Smith and Wesson from his waistband. In the yellow patch of light which

54

beamed down from the kitchen, he revolved the drum to check the load.

He slid the weapon back into place, then said to Loomis, 'Stay with Charl and the kids 'til I get back. I may be gone awhile.'

CHAPTER FIVE

He cut down alongside the barn, then moved through the line of adjacent yards. His damp clothes clung to him. He picked his way carefully, walking onto the flat to circle around a pile of tin cans and rubbish which soiled the earth behind one of the houses.

The flat was quiet and dark. He could not see anything except the few feet of sand ahead. He could hear only the whisper of the slight wind against the leaves of the cottonwoods that shaded the yards. Far to the east the pass which had meant so much safety until today was lost in the night's blackness, closed from his vision as clearly as it was closed to him and his family as a way of escape.

He and Charlotte had taken six days to come through Oursler's Pass because of the danger to their unborn child. They'd rested a night in the foothills, covered by grass and a few pines, so Charlotte could get her strength for the long climb. That night she'd had her first real feeling of safety since they'd left Texas. She'd talked

55

about it while she lay in their wagon and watched the sunlight fade and the darkness work up into the mountains above them. She'd become more and more secure after they'd topped the divide and climbed this second range, then started the descent along the narrow crooked trail of the pass. And they'd finally seen the Hole spread out before them.

The valley had seemed larger than he'd remembered. Hatchet Creek, which cut through toward the south, was spotted with aspens and cottonwoods clear to the small settlement. The hay that kept the farmers going was high and golden brown that summer. The Haycox and Oursler ranches which brought the farmers' hay were already rambling spreads that showed the prosperity Buffalo Hole could have. Cows, chickens, ducks, pigs and dogs had watched them from the farmyards as they'd driven in. Farmers and their children had waved from their hay and grain fields. The high sandstone cliffs in the north, the mountains which closed in the valley on all sides, completed their feeling of safety and contentment. They'd lain awake and talked and planned the first night in their hotel room. McKee had bought the land for his general store the very next day...

*　　　*　　　*

Tetterman was sitting at the registration desk

56

when McKee entered the lobby. The hotelman's high-cheeked face glanced up, then stared. Tetterman stood and stepped around the counter to intercept McKee before he reached the second-floor staircase.

'Where are you going?' the hotelman asked.

'I want to talk to Basso.'

Tetterman's eyes dropped to McKee's coatfront, flicked back to McKee's face. 'Mr Basso has some friends up there playing cards. He doesn't want to be disturbed.'

McKee moved past him and started up the stairs. Tetterman made no motion to stop him. He dogged along behind McKee, warning, 'You're just making trouble for yourself. Haycox and Royce are with Mr Basso.'

The skinny hotelman half-ran ahead of McKee once they were in the hallway. He reached the door of Basso's room first. He knocked.

'Come in,' said Basso's deep voice.

The room was filled with tobacco smoke. Half-empty liquor bottles and glasses lined the dresser. Piled on the bed which had been pushed into one corner were the hats and coats of the three men who sat with shirtsleeves rolled up around a card table. All watched Tetterman precede McKee into the room. Basso was in the chair which faced the door. He took his thin Mexican cigar from his mouth, waved a friendly hand at McKee. Haycox and Royce grinned, welcoming

57

McKee.

'Well, storekeeper,' said Basso. 'I'm glad you came in. Sit down and join the game.'

'I'm not here to play cards,' McKee said pointedly. 'I had to have my horse shot just now and you damn well know why.'

Tetterman warned, 'Watch him, Mr Basso. He's got a gun under his coat.'

Basso stared at McKee as if he was dumbfounded. He was calm, his hard tanned features beneath his bushy gray eyebrows completely controlled. Royce pushed his chair away from the table, the sharp scraping noise the only sound in the quiet room. Haycox's smile had vanished. His face was red and little drops of perspiration beaded his forehead from being in the hot room so long. The collar of his shirt was open, his black string tie hanging like an uneven, twisted shoelace. He laid his cards, face-down, on the table.

'What in hell are you trying?' he asked McKee.

'Basso knows. He'll tell you.'

Basso's head shook. He looked confused. His stare stayed on McKee, yet he spoke to Haycox. 'I have absolutely no idea of what he's talking about. Now do you see why I asked you to have the sheriff come up here, too? It wasn't enough he accused my men.'

'You had my horse's leg broken,' McKee began. 'You...'

'You are insane.' Basso gestured with the

cigar at Haycox and Royce. 'I've been right here in this room since we got back from Oursler's.' His deep-set eyes narrowed, but he remained calm. 'I'm getting tired of this, storekeeper. I came to Buffalo Hole to do business with the cattlemen here, not to have trouble with you.'

'You came here to kill me and my family. You brought those two gunhands with you to do the job.'

'Gunhands?' Basso mimicked. He suddenly looked very amused. 'I'll show you my gunhands.' He left the table and walked to the door of the adjoining room. When he opened it, McKee could see Cooley and Jonas, both coatless with shirtsleeves rolled up, seated at a table of their own playing cribbage. They glanced at their boss who said, 'Come in here, you men.'

Cooley entered the room first, then the huge man. They stopped beside the bed.

'All right, look at my gunhands.' Basso laughed. 'They haven't worn guns since you made trouble in your store. Mr Haycox and the sheriff know as well as I do that they've been in there all evening.'

'One of them went out, Basso. I don't know which one. One of them did. He tried to make it look like my horse kicked the stall, but he left mud on the floor.'

'Look at their boots,' said Basso. Both men lifted their boots, showed the soles and high

59

heels. Basso continued, 'There's no mud on them. Check their clothes. If either of them went out his clothes would be wet, or damp anyway.' He waved his cigar at the open doorway. 'Go on. Look inside the closet. See if you can find muddy boots or wet clothes.'

The man who'd hurt Queen had changed his clothes, McKee knew. The muddy boots and wet clothing wouldn't be in either room. He turned to Haycox and Royce. 'Nate, Queen's leg was broken by an iron bar during the storm. Basso had one of these two do it. I can't prove it, but it's true.'

'I'm gettin' damn sick of this,' Jonas said, moving toward McKee with his slow, flat-footed walk. 'I'm paid to protect Mr Basso. As far as I can see you're just out to cause him harm.'

'Hold it, Jonas,' Basso ordered. The huge man halted. Basso studied Haycox very carefully. 'I came here in good faith, Oakley. I want to do business in this valley. I can't have your people always causing trouble.'

Haycox motioned to the hall door and said irritably, 'Get out of here, McKee.'

'Not until this is settled.'

'It is settled. You ain't goin' to ruin everythin' I've worked for. I've even got Will Oursler to come in tomorrow ... Sheriff, what 'bout that gun under his coat. There's a no-gun law in this town.'

Royce held his hand out to McKee. 'Let me
60

have it, Ben.'

McKee hesitated.

Royce kept his right hand raised. 'Don't force me to take it. I will if I have to.'

'You're damned lucky Mr Basso hasn't asked Nate to lock you up,' Haycox snapped. 'You're so worried about your family you should've thought of that before you came bargin' in here.'

'No, I don't want him locked up,' said Basso. 'I just don't want trouble. I'm willing to forget this if I can be sure there won't be any more trouble.'

'There won't be,' Royce promised. He took a step closer to McKee. 'The gun. Now.'

McKee unbuttoned his coat and drew the Smith and Wesson. He handed it to the lawman.

Tetterman moved to the hall door and opened it. 'I'm really sorry this happened, Mr Basso. I really regret it.'

'That's all right,' Basso told him. He stood watching McKee intently, a steady patient frown on his face.

McKee turned away. He walked into the hall. Tetterman closed the door behind him.

'I don't want you in here again,' the hotelman said angrily. 'If I see you trying to get close to Mr Basso or his bodyguards, I'll send for the sheriff myself.'

McKee did not answer. He walked down the stairs, through the lobby, and onto the porch.

61

The night was dark and the sky was black and the town seemed to hold a hundred hiding places for Basso's men. His attempt to show he was willing to fight for his family's safety had proved nothing except that he was excessively small and alone and his family very vulnerable to Basso's next move.

He shivered as he stepped off the porch to walk home.

CHAPTER SIX

Hy Loomis opened the front door for him. McKee bent over to untie his shoelaces as soon as he was inside. He didn't want to track mud through the hallway. Charl worked too hard to keep the house clean ... He straightened when he heard Freddy say, 'What did you do to them, Pop?'

The boys stood at the top of the stairs with their mother. Charlotte looked pale and haggard. Freddy bit down on his lower lip to keep from crying. Tommy made no attempt to hold back what he felt. He rubbed his small fists into his swollen red eyes. He'd been crying for a long time.

'Charlotte had to tell them,' Loomis said in a soft voice. 'They saw Ramon's helper drive around back with his wagon.'

McKee nodded. 'Thanks. Thanks a lot, Hy.'

He reached into his trouser pocket and took out the store key. 'You open up in the morning. I may not be in 'til late.'

'Let me stay here. I can help.'

'I don't want you caught in this.' He looked toward the stairs. 'It's bad enough with them in it. Be careful, though. Watch yourself while you go home.'

Loomis put on his hat and slicker. When he was gone, McKee walked up the stairs.

'You got them, didn't you, Pop?' said Tommy. 'You got even for what they did to Queen?'

'They won't bother us tonight,' he told them. 'You two better get your sleep now.'

The boys turned in to their room. Charlotte paused to talk to him. McKee glanced after their sons. 'Get them under the covers,' he said quietly. 'I'll stop in when I get these wet things off.'

He closed the door of his bedroom while he changed into dry pants and shirt. The door to Maryann's room was open. The baby slept peacefully in her crib. After he was dressed McKee took a few minutes to hurriedly clean and load the Winchester carbine. He returned to the hallway. He leaned the weapon against the wall before he stepped into the boys' room.

'Dad,' Fred said. 'They'll tell us where they bury Queen, won't they?'

'I can ask Mr Lerrazza.'

'We can get a stone or somethin', can't we?

63

And put it on the grave?'

'Yes, of course. I'll ask Mr Lerrazza. You boys sleep now.'

He kissed his sons good night. He and Charlotte walked out of the room. He purposely left the hallway lamp on when they went down the stairs. Charlotte eyed the Winchester as he picked it up to carry with him. She did not speak until they were in the kitchen and he had set the carbine on the table.

'You didn't have your revolver when you got home.'

'Royce took it. I was lucky he didn't take me in. He would have if Basso had pressed charges.'

She backed toward the sinkboard, her expression grim and intent. She still talked in a hushed voice. 'What's the matter with Royce? I thought he was our friend. That he respected you. He should've arrested those men the first time you accused them.'

McKee sighed. 'They haven't done anything he can hold them for. Not legally.'

'Don't "not legally" me. We know what they did.'

'But we have no proof. Basso made me look ridiculous in that hotel.' He explained everything. She listened intently, did not interrupt. He watched her, suddenly realizing how worn she'd become. Today in the store he'd felt a personal pride in her youthful appearance, at the way she looked consistently in her twenties and, when she was especially happy, more like a gay high-schooler. Now, her shoulders were slumped, her face drawn, almost gaunt.

'And Haycox made him take your gun?'

'Nate had to. He loses Haycox's backing in an election, he'd be out of his job. With his wife sick...'

'So now Basso can roam this town and pick his own way to harm us. Who do you think he'll try for next? Tommy, or Maryann? Or me? The only thing we do know is that he wants you last.'

'Please, Charlotte, sweetheart. Please.'

'You "please." You do something. You're the father in this family. You were such a great lawman. You were such a strong man with a gun, you got us into this.'

'That was my job.'

'I know it was. It still would be if a drunken cowhand hadn't gone after you.' She took a step toward him, glaring at him fiercely. 'I almost died once. I didn't bring my babies into the world to have a hate-filled man murder them.'

'I didn't either.'

Her hand was raised to him. He made no movement to avoid anything she might do. Then, her building hysteria crumbled and he had her in his arms. Her body trembled. He held her, and she quieted. She spoke against his neck.

65

'I almost hated ... I could kill them for what they're doing to us.'

'I know. I ought to let you and Tom go up there.'

She tried to smile but couldn't. He held her close.

'You have every reason to feel like this, Charl. I do myself. I wanted to draw my gun and shoot Basso and his two gunmen in that hotel room. I wanted to do that when I went up with Nate this afternoon. I was a strong man with a gun once. I haven't lost that instinct. But I realize what I'd be doing to us. I'd end up on a gallows or in prison. Then, I can't be positive, sweetheart. I might only get two of them. The third would be walking around free, out here with you and the kids.'

She shook her head. 'Oh, Lord. Dear, Lord,' she said softly. 'I'm not strong, Ben. I'm not. I'm sorry, but I'm not.'

'There's no strong way to handle this. If I thought we could've gotten through the pass, I'd've packed us up before they crippled poor Queen. Either that, or I'd've taken you and the kids up to the rock cabin. That's what I think Basso wanted at first. He would have used guns outside of town. Now he's enjoying it more this way. My guess is that he won't use guns if we stay right here. He won't rush us. The main thing for us is to be careful.'

She nodded, listening.

'I can't be positive about the guns, though.

66

You know a little about how to use this carbine. I'll show you and the boys in the morning. I'll get a Colt and a derringer from the store. You'll carry the derringer.'

'I'll use it if I have to. I will.'

He tilted her chin so she looked into his face. 'Only if you have to. We'll stay close together, all of us. We won't give them a chance to get one of us alone.' He kissed the tip of her nose. 'You know what I like,' he added, touching the bobbed end. 'The round part, right here.'

She linked her fingers in his. 'I'm going up,' she said. 'You come up.'

'In a few minutes. After I check the house.'

He watched her go along the hallway. She seemed more confident, he felt. Yet he did not feel the confidence he'd expressed to her. He took the Winchester from the table and levered a cartridge into the chamber. Then he moved from window to window and to the doors, testing the locks. The sky was very dark, the low clouds still thick and heavy. The chances were good this time of year that they would break away before dawn.

He checked the last window lock, turned it hard to make certain it couldn't be jimmied loose. He walked slowly up the stairs to where his precious children were sound asleep.

CHAPTER SEVEN

McKee hardly slept all night. He and Charlotte lay awake talking in whispers until she dozed off. Ben was up at the slightest hint of noise. He paced the house, stopping often at the windows to listen. The sky cleared toward morning and the wind calmed. When the first light of daybreak showed beyond the eastern rim, he built a fire, then stayed down in the kitchen to shave. The cold water and lather took the sleepiness from him as he honed his straight edge on the worn cowhide strap which hung below the mirror. Ten years of work inside the store had faded the weather-hardness out of his skin. He shaved with short, careful strokes. As carefully, he trimmed the graying hair where it fuzzed against the tops of his ears. He'd planned to bring the boys with him to the barber's around noon. That would have to wait now.

His family slept until Maryann woke at ten past eight. Charlotte was up with the baby. In just a few minutes the boys heard their talk. The sun was a red arc above the rim. Mist rose from the wet ground, a thin whiteness that shifted and drifted in the slight breeze, partially hiding from view the cattle which grazed far out on the level flat of the Hole. At breakfast they had a short discussion on the fury of the thunder storm. Nobody spoke of Queen. Fred planned what they'd do during the town celebration that afternoon. He tried to be exuberant for his smaller brother's sake, but Tommy was silent. The reddish hollows were still under his eyes.

'We'll get Billy Royce and climb up on the jail roof like we did last year,' Fred said. 'We'll watch the fireworks from there.'

'No, you won't,' McKee told them. 'We'll stay close together, the five of us. We don't leave each other for any reason.'

'Gee, Dad. Can't we all go up on the jail roof. Billy's father won't mind.'

'Can you see your mother climbing up onto the roof?' McKee said, smiling.

They all laughed, and McKee said, 'You help Mom clean the dishes and the house. After, I want to show you how to handle the Winchester. I'll have it in good working condition by then.'

He cleaned the carbine while the boys helped their mother. The kitchen shade was kept drawn during the gun-handling lesson. The first rule was that the boys weren't to touch the weapon unless it was absolutely necessary. Only if Basso's threat came into the house, only if their father or their mother couldn't handle the situation. Pumping the carbine was second nature to the boys who'd learned with toy guns. They had mainly to get used to the heavier weight. Charlotte lost her

69

awkwardness after a few directions from McKee. Her face was set in a frown of concentration. There was a deadly seriousness about her McKee had never seen before. The children also sensed it. The boys, even Maryann, were much quieter than usual.

'I'll keep the carbine on the mantle of the fireplace,' McKee said. 'There it'll be out of Maryann's reach.'

'Suppose we're upstairs?' Fred asked.

'I'll bring home a Colt from the store tonight. We'll keep that upstairs.' McKee glanced at the wall clock. 'It's almost ten-thirty. You kids wash and finish dressing so we can be out before noon.'

Fred began to pump water into the basin. Charlotte put the kettle on the stove. She said, 'I hate to take a good time away from them, but we would be safer if we stayed home.'

'No. We're safer out with the rest of the people today. Basso isn't going to do anything in the open. If we stayed in here, we wouldn't dare to pass a window.'

'Hey, Tommy, come on,' Fred called. 'Your turn to wash.' He'd splashed water on his face and now stood watching his brother at the window.

Ben and Charlotte stepped close to Tommy. The small boy turned to them and said angrily, 'We could get another horse and put her in the barn. I'd sit here and wait. Anyone tried to get in there, I'd shoot him.'

70

Fred said, 'No. Not yet. I don't want another horse in there yet.'

'I don't want another horse either,' answered Tommy. 'I just want to kill the man who killed Queen.'

McKee put his hand on Tommy's shoulder. 'We all want to have the man pay. He will, when Sheriff Royce learns who did it.' He gave him a small push. 'Come on. Wash up.'

Tommy moved to the sinkboard. McKee said quietly to Charlotte, 'I don't like the way it's affecting them. I didn't want to teach them how to handle that carbine. I thought about it all during the night. There was no other way. If anything happened to us...' He stared through the glass at the half-open barn door. 'It is the best thing that we go out. Maybe I can force Basso to do something in the open. Royce would have to act then.'

Charlotte looked dubious. 'I don't know...'

'I know,' McKee said. 'I'll be careful how I do it. I'll pick my time. Just make certain if there is trouble you get the kids safe out of the way.'

*   *   *

This last Saturday in August was the biggest day of the year in Buffalo Hole. It had started as the final shopping day before the new school term began. Farmers and ranchers came in to buy clothes and school articles for their

71

children. Friends who hadn't seen each other in weeks got together, new families were introduced to the older residents, equipment and supplies were bought for the winter months. The celebration idea had developed six years ago, when groups started gathering at one home or another. The first year a square dance was held, and after that something special had been planned: a Texas-style barbecue, a band concert, the band brought in by stage all the way from Denver, even a Mexican fiesta with brightly colored costumes and a three-man guitar-and-accordion group formed by Ramon Lerrazza for the dancing. This year a box lunch would be held when the stores closed at five. After the children were put to bed, there would be a square dance for the adults.

The five McKees left their house a few minutes before twelve. Already the hot sun had sucked the water of the night's storm from the earth, leaving a thin white dust which kicked up in tiny powdery bursts at each footstep. Heat waves rose visibly over the hay fields and cattle that fed on the sparse grass far out along the flat. McKee had repeated his orders about the family staying close together. He carried Maryann beside Charlotte who held the box lunch. The two boys kept only a step ahead of them. The town was crowded with people going in and out of the stores. Groups stood on porches and walks while they conversed. Small boys chased each other around the legs of the grown-ups. Friends of the McKees called to them, then stopped and talked for a few minutes before they moved on to continue their shopping. It was almost one o'clock when the family passed the buckboard and two farmer's wagons which were tied at the general store hitchrails.

Fred slowed before he started up onto the store porch. He glanced down Main toward their home. 'I don't know what's happened to Billy Royce,' he remarked. 'He said he'd be at our house by noon.'

'His mother probably needed him at home,' Charlotte said. 'You know how she's been feeling.'

Fred nodded and went up the stairs. McKee stopped once he was inside the screen door. He lowered Maryann to the floor and spoke to the boys. 'Remember, you don't go out until I close the store.'

'Sure, Pop,' said Tommy. He took just two steps up the side aisle before he halted. 'Pop. What's the matter? The gun case's empty.'

McKee looked across the counters into the iron-barred glass case. Every weapon he'd put on display was gone. He turned toward the dry-goods section. Hy Loomis, who'd been waiting on two women, waved at McKee. The short fat clerk spoke quickly to the women. He left them talking together while they felt the cloth of several bolts on the counter in front

73

of them.

'Ben,' he said when he reached the McKees. 'You saw the gun case. Royce came in 'bout an hour ago and took all the guns and ammunition. He says he's holdin' them 'til that Basso leaves.'

'He didn't leave any here to sell?'

Loomis' round bald head shook. 'He said if you had a sale, you could go over to the jail. I couldn't stop him. He said he had a legal right to do it. I couldn't go down to your house after you because of the customers.'

'That's all right. Just keep handling things. Charlotte and the kids will stay here until we close up.'

Loomis headed back to his customers. McKee said, 'Tom, Fred. I'm going over to the jail for a few minutes. You'll keep close to Maryann while Mom helps Mr Loomis.'

'Okay. Sure, Dad.'

McKee looked at Charlotte. 'This might be exactly what we want. If Basso made any charges, I'll make sure the whole town knows it.'

Her eyes were wide, fearful. 'You'll be out there without a gun. If Basso means to start trouble, you can be killed.'

'He doesn't mean to start trouble. Not any that people can see.'

'You can't be sure.'

'I'll be all right. I'm doing the right thing, don't worry.' He walked to the screen door.

After he was outside he glanced around. She still stood where he'd left her. He'd thought this morning when she'd learned how to use the Winchester that she had more confidence. There was no confidence in her face now. She looked small, tired and dreadfully afraid.

* * *

He crossed Main Street directly to the jail.

The sheriff's office was empty, but the door which led to the jail block was open. McKee walked to it and gazed down the small corridor between the outer wall and the floor-to-ceiling iron bars of the three cells. Nate Royce stood in the last cubicle. He'd piled two boxes of McKee's guns beside the door. The loose weapons and ammunition that he'd taken from the showcase lay on the bunk. He turned at the sound of McKee's footsteps.

'How come you took those guns, Nate?' McKee asked.

The answer came too quickly, the answer of a man who was irritated or nervous, or possibly both. 'I figured it would be safer all around if I had them. You know the county laws. I have a right to impound any weapon if I believe the owner can become a threat to the community.'

'All right. If Basso's made charges, I want them brought out into the open.'

'Basso didn't make any charges. I'm doin'

75

this on my own.'

'You're doing it for Haycox then.'

'I'm doing it for your own good.' Royce gestured impatiently, ran one hand through his thinning black hair. 'I'm tryin' to keep you from bein' locked up in here. If I left a gun in your store, you'd put one on and go after Basso.' He glanced at the weapons on the bunk. 'That's what I want to keep from happenin'.'

'Nate, the only thing you're trying to keep is your job.'

That brought Royce's glance back, his lips parted in anger. 'Dammit, can't you see? Basso had you last night. One word from him and I'd've had to take you in. You went after him with a gun, a man as big as Basso. He's no phoney. Haycox checked on him after he got his first letter three months ago. He owns the Basso Cattle and Land Company. He can back up everything he claims. He's put other places like this town really on their feet. The things he wants to do for the Hole, he's done somewhere else. Haycox checked on that, and it's true.'

'Nate, I helped arrest Giles Basso in New Mexico eighteen years ago. No matter what he's got now, he is that man. He's here to kill every member of my family. You can check on him. The Albuquerque prison will have a record on him.'

Their stares met. The sheriff broke the exchange by looking away. 'I don't have time

76

for that. Basso plans to leave on the stage next week. He's over in the Stockman's right now, drawin' up contracts for Haycox and Oursler. I mean to see he gets out alive. I'm keepin' these guns. If I see you carryin' one, I'll arrest you.'

Royce wiped his mouth with the back of his hand. He added in a softer voice, 'Look ... Basso hasn't said one word against you. His bodyguards aren't even packin' guns. Just stay out of his way 'til he leaves. I'll watch your house if you want me to.'

'That's all you'll do,' McKee said.

'That's all I can do.'

'Well, I'll do everything I can to protect my family,' McKee answered. He waited. This time Royce merely watched him impassively. McKee started to turn. Then Royce said, 'Tell Fred and Tom that Billy won't be out today. His mother was worse this morning and she needs him. I know the kids had planned...'

'They'll understand,' McKee stated flatly. 'They know what it feels like to need help.'

Outside McKee hurried across the dusty street, heedless of the people he passed. He could expect no help as long as Haycox controlled the sheriff. With a sick wife at home, the job was too important, too necessary to Royce. A homesteader's wagon rumbled past him. A bearded farmer and his calico-dressed wife waved to McKee. Their four kids, piled atop the produce they'd brought into town to trade, yelled to their school friends. McKee waved, hearing the safe, contented laughter and talk of the people. The sun threw a burning heat. The evening would come and they'd hold their celebration. All this, he told himself, was reality. Day, night, the happy town. And inside his store the only reality for his family was the incredible threat which hung over them.

The Winchester in his house was good only if Basso came there after them. That was improbable. McKee tried to think of where he could get a revolver. Ten, even five years ago, it would have been a simple request to one of his neighbors. But since the no-gun law had been passed, most of the men had gotten rid of their weapons. The old, wild days were gone. There was no need for a person to have a gun. McKee gazed at the faces close by as he walked up the steps of the general store. He wasn't sure he should ask anyone. It could bring the man who did the lending under Basso's threat.

He pushed past the screen door.

He halted. He stood motionless, the tips of his fingers still holding the door. Giles Basso walked toward him from the direction of the front counters. He held two small bags in his hand, smoked a thin black Mexican cigar. He wore the well-pressed black broadcloth and black Stetson. A wide smile was on his face.

McKee let go of the door. Basso walked slowly, casually, taking his time to reach McKee. His smile did not change.

'What do you want in here?' McKee kept his

voice low.

'I'm shopping. I bought myself some pipe tobacco and some Mexican cigars.'

'I don't want you in my store.'

Basso's smile widened as if he hadn't heard. 'You know I haven't been able to get these cigars this far north. I'm very glad I've found a place to buy them.'

'I don't want you in here. Or your two gunhands.'

'Nice store you've got, Mr McKee.' He waved the cigar back at the side and rear counters. 'Nice. I'd say you've really got everything you want right here.'

McKee looked across Basso's shoulder and saw Charlotte with three women customers at the dress counter. She watched them, her lips pressed tight. Tommy and Fred talked to two boys at the cracker barrel. Maryann was busy eating a cookie near Loomis, who was grinding coffee for a farm woman.

'Damn you, Basso. I'm not going to stand...'

'Go ahead. One free punch and you're in jail. I won't fight you, Sheriff. Go ahead.'

McKee stared at his half-raised right fist. His fingers uncurled and his arm dropped to his side. 'What do you really want? Why are you dragging things out like this?'

The deep-set black eyes narrowed, but the smile still exposed the even line of strong white teeth. 'It won't drag out for eighteen years,

79

Sheriff. No, not that long. I just want you to feel a little of what it's like. I had fifteen years in a prison to think about two boys who were killed by you. They were both under twenty. Did you know that?'

'They were young.'

'Eighteen and nineteen. We'd lost our ranch in that drought of 'eighty-three. We needed the money so we could buy another spread. We figured a small bank would have enough. We didn't figure on two lawmen in a town that small. That's how green we were. We didn't even check on the lawmen. We were so green, you couldn't miss us.'

'You could've thrown down your guns when we gave you the chance. You kept shooting.'

Basso shook his head. 'I wasn't green when I got out of prison. You know the people you meet in prison, Sheriff? Well, they know how to plan things.'

'Basso, I don't want to stand here like this.'

'You will, though. Because if you don't, I'll smash out that window. You get the idea, Sheriff. I'll claim you attacked me and I'll have you in jail in less than two minutes. It won't be so much fun for me that way, but I'll do what I want while you're locked up. You think I can't do it?'

They stared at each other. Basso's smile was gone. He was entirely at ease in the knowledge that he controlled the situation. 'I made plans, Sheriff, for Hutchins and you. I knew how to

80

take a bank. That's what I did. One month after I got out, I held up a bank. I got fifty-eight thousand dollars, Sheriff. With that money I knew I could do what I wanted.'

'And you wanted Hutchins and me?'

'Now you know what you're saying. I started a cattle-buying business. I spent a whole year building up the business. So I'd be legitimate, Sheriff. I made some good deals in New Mexico. Made friends. Then I went to that little town where you killed my two boys. And I learned Hutchins was dead.'

McKee started to speak. Basso went on quickly. 'I traced you, Sheriff. From Don Pedro to Hays City to Amarillo. And I came up here and started doing business. You know, I've given three valleys within a hundred miles of here the same deal I offered Haycox and Oursler? I made sure I contacted people Haycox and Oursler would know, so when I wrote to them my plan wouldn't miss. It didn't miss. I even got Oursler so interested he's coming into town to see me. The part about you and your family can't fail. See now, you aren't facing green kids like my two boys. I want you to know that. And no matter how long I decide to drag this out, I won't fail.'

Basso did not wait for an answer. He put the cigar between his lips and pushed the door open. He moved off the porch and along the boardwalk. He did not look back.

Charlotte hurried down the aisle and

81

stopped beside McKee. 'I didn't notice him come in. I finished waiting on Mrs Rand and he was next in line. I didn't know what to do when I saw him.'

'What did he say to you?'

'He didn't say much. He was so polite, and he kept smiling. He bought tobacco and some cheroots. He watched the children, Ben, and he kept smiling. That smile. He isn't just a gunman trying to get even. That man isn't sane.'

'I don't think he is either.'

Her face was solemn, thoughtful. 'What about the box lunch? Do you think we should go home?'

He glanced toward where Tommy and Fred busily talked to their friends. Maryann still sat beside Hy Loomis, the chocolate from her cookie smeared all over her small round face.

'We're safe in a crowd. The boys have planned on this for so long. We'll wait until some of the other parents start taking their kids home. We'll stay with them. Unless you're too afraid.'

Charlotte stared out through the window. Basso had crossed Main into the hotel. 'I'll be afraid no matter where we are.' She breathed in deeply. 'This morning when you taught us how to load and handle the gun ... I wanted to learn. I had to, but I kept wondering if I could aim it at a man and pull the trigger. I really saw what Basso is just now. I don't wonder any more. I know I can.'

CHAPTER EIGHT

The last three hours of the business day were very busy. The store was continually crowded with customers lined up two and three deep at the counters. McKee kept Charlotte and Hy Loomis working at the back and side shelves and counters where they could watch the children. Ben handled the sales at the front near the window. Here he was able to see everything that went on outside. If Basso or his men did attempt to come close to his family, he was in a position to meet them before they got past the porch door.

McKee knew the last thing Basso wanted now was direct action. He'd drag out what he meant to do just as long as he could, the way a cat pawed a cornered mouse. He'd known exactly what effect his visit to the store would have on Charlotte. Each smile, each remark, had been calculated to wear her nerves thin. His long drawn-out talk, explaining in minute detail the steps he'd taken to get Haycox and Oursler in a position where they'd back him, had been aimed at building the same reaction within McKee. The twisted state of Basso's mind demanded that the McKees suffer as he had in prison. He'd choose his own time to stop his pawing at them, and then he'd pounce. But McKee didn't feel it would come from this open street.

Still he couldn't be certain. He kept a close watch through the window. He had a good idea of exactly who was in town. He saw white-haired Will Oursler ride past in a buggy driven by his foreman. He watched Haycox meet Oursler in front of the Stockman's building. The two ranchers went inside together. They hadn't come out by the time the final shopper left the general store at five-thirty. McKee closed and locked the door. He lowered the wide green window shade.

Hy Loomis was at the rolltop desk behind the rear counter checking the charge slips. Charlotte waited near the cracker barrel with Maryann and the boys. The room looked bare now that all the shelves and counters were practically empty of merchandise.

'Forget that, Hy,' McKee said. 'Come along to the town hall with us.'

'I'm almost through,' the clerk told him. 'I'll be in before the dancin' starts.'

'Come on, Dad,' Fred said. He held up the box which contained the family lunch. 'We'll be late for the bidding.'

'Yuh, Pop. C'mon,' echoed Tommy.

'Okay. Okay.' McKee grinned. 'You'd think you guys hadn't eaten since this morning.' Both boys laughed. Charlotte smiled, but she kept turning her wedding band around and

84

around on her finger. McKee leaned over and picked up Maryann. 'Okay, here we go,' he said. 'Remember, now. We stay close. We don't leave each other all the time this shindig is going on.'

*   *   *

Thick shadows crawled across Main from the west side false fronts. The windows glowed warmly, reflecting the last rays of the red circle of sun low over the distant peaks. Most of the people were already at the town hall. Only a few moved along the walk ahead of the McKees to where an orderly line waited on the long front porch to go inside. The building was a two-story wooden structure. All the county offices, with the exception of the jail, were on the second floor. A large community hall took up the entire bottom section. Loud chatter of women and happy children's laughter came through the open windows.

Fred started to walk faster, stepping out in front of Tommy when they were still a block away. McKee said, 'Hold it, Fred. We'll have plenty of time.' The boy slowed, allowed his family to catch up. McKee studied the adults who crowded the doorway. Neither Basso nor his two men were in sight.

They took their place in line. They talked and waved to friends. The boys shouted to other boys while they moved into the hall.

McKee hardly heard what was said. His eyes scanned the gathering, then rested on the small stage at the front of the long room. Basso sat beside Haycox in the center of the platform. The four other members of the town council and Sheriff Royce filled the rest of the chairs.

But Cooley and Jonas were not in sight.

Worriedly, McKee thought of his home. Basso could have had one of them go to the house and set up something for when the family returned. He followed Charlotte past the occupied chairs of the middle section. He'd have to find a good reason to leave a short while after the eating began. He could run home and check before he let anyone go inside. It would have to be a plausible excuse, so he wouldn't alarm Charlotte or the kids.

He saw Basso's two men just as the boys sighted six empty chairs. Cooley and Jonas stood smoking with a group of townsmen beyond the open side doorway. Both were busy in conversation and paid no attention to the McKees. Basso hadn't so much as glanced in McKee's direction.

'Say, Ben, shift your chairs around,' Ted Gilmartin called. 'We can have our families sit together.'

'Sure, Ted. Here, boys. Move these chairs.'

Charlotte took Maryann, then sat beside Rose Gilmartin to talk. Ted was McKee's age, a talkative man who owned the restaurant. He was a big person, prematurely gray. His wife was a tall, dark-haired woman with a perpetual smile that never left her mouth. Ben and Charlotte liked the Gilmartins. The two couples often got together during the winter to play whist.

'Heard your mare broke her leg,' Gilmartin said to Ben.

'Yes.' McKee gazed at where Tommy and Fred sat with Gilmartin's two boys. They couldn't hear. 'We think the leg was broken on purpose.'

'How? Why would anyone do that?'

'Well, we've had trouble the past couple days.' He stopped talking for the crowd had started to quiet. Oakley Haycox was standing at his chair. He waved his arms in front of him, asking for silence. Behind him four men were moving a table piled high with box lunches onto the center of the stage.

All talk died. The men who'd been on the side porch stepped in through the doorway and lined themselves along the wall.

'This is a fine turnout,' Haycox said. 'It looks as if the whole county is right here in this room. And that's exactly how it should be.'

Two beagle hounds that had trailed the men inside from the porch started barking, as if loudly agreeing with the cattleman's words. Laughter broke out and a few good-humored remarks were called to Haycox. The laughter toned down.

Haycox grinned. 'As I said, this is exactly as

87

it should be. We have a good friendly community here, and it's spirit like this that'll keep us growin'.' He paused to glance at the dogs, both still near the door, but quiet. 'We'll get to the box social in a few minutes. First, I want to take this time to introduce Mr Giles Basso, the owner of the Basso Land and Cattle Company.'

He half-turned and motioned with his right hand at Basso. Basso gave a slight nod of his head.

Haycox went on. 'Mr Basso came here with an offer to buy and handle our cattle for the next five years. It's a wonderful thing for the valley, the best thing that's ever happened to us. Will Oursler and I have been drawin' up contracts with Mr Basso. Will's in the Stockman's now, readin' the small print. Soon as we finish signin', we'll give you all the particulars. I can tell you one thing. Every last person in Buffalo Hole'll profit by this.' Small talk hummed here and there in the audience. Haycox gestured for silence. 'Now, I told Mr Basso and the men who are with him that they'd see a real family-type time here. So you show them. I know you'll show them.'

He turned to the table and took one of the top containers, a shoe box tied with a bright red ribbon.

He held the box high for everyone to see. 'Now, before I start auctioneerin', I want to remind you that all the money we take in goes for new books for the school library. So don't hold back.' He circled the box above his head. 'How am I bid for this fine, heavy dinner?'

'Four bits,' a voice said at the rear of the hall.

Haycox nodded. 'Pike Lott says fifty cents. Do I hear any more bids?'

'Better not,' Pike Lott, a tall, gangling hay farmer, spoke up. 'That belongs to my missus, and she said she'd skin me if I didn't buy it.'

More laughter, shrieks from the children. Before it calmed, Giles Basso stood at his chair.

'Mr Haycox,' he said, laughingly. 'I'd like to take part in this.' He stared friendlily toward the rear of the hall. 'If Mr Lott and his wife don't mind. I know that school fund can use money. I'll bid fifty dollars for that box on the condition the Lotts will do me the honor of eating with me.'

'Wal, you sure can,' Lott called. He grinned, put his half-dollar back into his pocket. Basso began to come down the stage steps.

Someone clapped for Basso, than more clapping. Basso halted on the bottom step. 'I have two business associates with me,' he said. 'If you don't mind, they'll bid as they see fit and join you fine people in your celebration.'

The clapping continued until Haycox held up the next box. McKee watched Basso walk up the side aisle, a wide smile on the cattlebuyer's face. Basso did not look toward the McKees until he was even with their chairs. For a brief moment his eyes flicked to the left, first resting on the children and Charlotte, then on McKee. Basso's smile held and he was gone behind them.

'Our second box,' Haycox announced from the stage. 'It's a big one. Who'd like to start the biddin'?'

Charlotte leaned close to Ben. 'What is Basso doing?' she said.

'I don't know. He could be enjoying this. Don't worry.'

Charlotte sat back in her chair to watch the auction. McKee tried to relax but couldn't. Basso had timed his actions too well, had made his speech too capably for it not to be part of his threat. McKee sat tensely, waiting for something to happen.

CHAPTER NINE

He did not have to wait long. He bought Charlotte's box for a dollar. Rose Gilmartin's was held up by Haycox a few minutes later. Ted Gilmartin bid one dollar.

Haycox raised the box above his head. 'Come on, one of you single men,' he said. 'You've been eatin' Rose Gilmartin's cookin' long enough to know you'll get plenty more than a dollar's worth.'

'I'll give twenty dollars,' a voice called from the side of the room. It was Jonas Foss who'd made the bid. He stood in front of the other men, a grin on his broad face. 'I had dinner at the restaurant. I know what I'm gettin'.'

'What do you say, Ted?' asked Haycox. 'You want to better that?'

Gilmartin stood, smiling. McKee touched his arm. 'Go to twenty-five, Ted. I'll pay the rest.'

'What? For my own wife's cooking?' He laughed and cut off anything McKee could add with, 'We'll share it with that man. Best advertisement we've had for our place this year.'

Jonas walked toward the stage to get his box. Charlotte had her lunch out, had already given Maryann a sandwich. Tommy and Fred waited beside her for theirs. Charlotte hesitated.

'What'll we do, Ben?'

McKee glanced around the room. All of the chairs were taken. Most of the people were eating. One of the small, short-legged beagle hounds that had barked at Haycox ran from group to group begging food. McKee looked at Tommy and Fred. 'All right, boys. Eat up. Watch out for the dog. He'll steal it from you.'

Charlotte said, 'I don't want that man eating with us.'

'He won't be with us. He'll stay with Ted's family.'

Charlotte handed each boy a sandwich. 'Stay right here,' she told them. 'Right next to me and your father.'

Jonas had reached the Gilmartins and was saying something about Rose's ability to cook. Sandwiches were passed out and they began to eat. Jonas did not even look toward the McKees.

McKee watched the huge man. Jonas did not make a move to come close to his family. From time to time McKee glanced around at Basso. Basso laughed and joked with the Lotts. He paid no attention to anyone else.

The groups which had started their lunches earliest finished first. A few of the men began lining the chairs against the walls to clear the floor for the dance. Charlotte gave Maryann and the boys their cookies. She sat the baby between her brothers.

'Watch her, Fred, while I get these napkins into the box.'

She crumbled the napkins and looked at McKee. He said, 'Come on, kids, we'll go now.'

The boys stood. Fred went to take Maryann's hand, but the baby reached for a chocolate cookie which lay on the seat of a close chair.

'No, no,' Fred said. 'Dirty, Maryann, dirty.' He bent to pick up the cookie.

The short-legged beagle hound slid in under Fred's hand and took the cookie in its mouth. The dog's pendulous ears shook while it chewed.

92

McKee gripped Maryann's small hand. Charlotte and the boys turned to walk up the aisle.

The dog's sudden bark made them halt. The animal barked again wildly, then whined. Those close by interrupted their conversation to watch. The dog started to run in circles, whining crazily and trying to bite at her side.

Ted Gilmartin went close to the animal. He reached out to help, but the beagle snapped viciously at him. The dog screamed in agony, rolled on the floor, writhing and making wild, pain-racked noises McKee had never heard before.

Ramon Lerrazza pushed through the crowd. Children watched with wide, terrified eyes. Some were crying. Lerrazza bent over the beagle. The animal made less noise now. Within a half-minute she lay still. The dark-skinned liveryman straightened. 'I think this dog's been poisoned,' he said.

McKee lifted Maryann and gave her to Charlotte. He stepped close to Lerrazza. 'You sure, Ramon?'

The Mexican nodded. 'Yes, I am sure. A strong poison, she died so quick.'

McKee's eyes searched the floor for bits of cookie the dog hadn't eaten. He found none. He said to Lerrazza, 'She was eating a cookie. I saw her.' He looked directly at Jonas, who stood with Rose and Ted Gilmartin. McKee said to the huge man, 'You were standing near where the dog picked up that cookie.'

'What?' Jonas' great shoulders hunched. 'Are you crazy? I was eatin' with these people.'

'You knew he was,' Ted Gilmartin said. 'What are you getting at, Ben?'

'You asked me about Queen, Ted. Her leg was broken with an iron bar. This dog's been poisoned. Both things happened since Basso and his men reached town.'

Behind him a voice murmured. Another answered. More talk grew on his left. Jonas' eyes narrowed, but his voice was calm. 'Look, you've been tryin' to cause trouble with Mr Basso since we got here. You can spread that phoney story 'bout him all you want. But you better not go pushin' me into anythin'.' He gazed at the Gilmartins. 'I didn't leave these people. I didn't give your dog anythin' to eat. I didn't even see the dog.'

'That cookie was left where it could be picked up by a child. Basso saw my daughter eating one like it in the store today.'

Haycox stepped in between the two men. 'What are you tryin', McKee? That cookie came from your store.'

'And I didn't buy it,' Jonas said. 'You go 'head, storekeeper. You think if I bought anythin' in your store.'

McKee could see the watching, waiting faces. The murmur of talk had silenced. He shook his head. 'I don't know who bought the cookie. I know it was dropped there so my
94

baby might pick it up. Only that poor animal ate it.'

Jonas nodded, the picture of patience. 'You made some pretty strong accusations against Mr Basso. He's a good man who don't want trouble. I'm not like that, storekeeper.'

'Your boss, Basso ...' McKee began.

'Leave him out of this. He was in the back of the hall. He still is. This is between you and me. You want to accuse me of poisonin' that dog, go 'head. Go 'head.'

McKee saw the watchers start to edge back. Women and children in the front pressed against the men. This was planned, too, he thought. He had no proof Jonas had put the cookie on the chair. He couldn't fight with all the women and kids here ...

'We'll see what Ramon says about the poison,' he said. He turned, nodded for Charlotte to go ahead of him with Maryann and the boys.

Talk broke out around McKee. He followed his family.

'Come on,' Jonas roared. 'Make your accusation. Either that or stop talkin' 'bout Mr Basso. Stop tryin' to ruin what he's doin' for this basin.'

McKee kept walking. The talk was louder. The men at the door opened a path for Charlotte. McKee stepped out onto the porch. Hy Loomis was near Fred and Tommy. The fat clerk stared across McKee's shoulder.

'He's comin' out after you, Ben,' Hy warned. 'Watch him.'

'Get Charl and the kids clear,' McKee said. 'Stay with them.'

Charlotte turned. 'Ben . . .'

'Go with Hy. Take the kids.'

Behind McKee, Jonas' voice was louder, nastier. 'Storekeeper, you gonna put up or shut up?' He grabbed McKee's shoulder and spun him around.

The men who'd crowded onto the porch fanned out in a semi-circle. The women and children had been blocked inside. Basso stood with the whiskered Cooley in the doorway. Basso smiled lazily. His glance wandered along the line of faces, judging their reactions. McKee kept his stare on the cattle buyer. He wanted the people to recognize the important enemy, so there would be no doubt it was Basso who controlled what Jonas was doing.

'It's about time you let this come out into the open, Basso,' he said.

'I don't see how I can stop it,' Basso answered. 'You've made a serious charge against Jonas. He has a right to force this.'

'Oh, no,' McKee said. 'You don't get out of it that easy.'

'He's not in this,' Jonas roared. 'You called me, storekeeper. Now back it up.'

McKee ignored him. 'When you control a man, Basso,' he said, calm and steady, 'you're responsible for his actions.'

96

Basso shook his head. 'I've held my men from going after you twice. Everyone here knows Jonas is innocent. I think you deserve a beating this time.'

'Damn right,' Jonas shouted. He took a step closer to McKee. McKee expected the huge man would start swinging, but he did not. Jonas stood with his thick nose inches away, his big fists ready. Disgustedly, he laughed into McKee's face. 'You were a lawman. No wonder Mr Basso had to hire bodyguards, if you're any example.'

McKee caught the hiss of drawn breaths. Beyond Jonas' back, Basso's smile might have been painted on. This was their aim, to humiliate him before everyone, the townsmen, his close friends, his family ... His stomach cramped, he felt the quickened beat of his pulse, the mounting cold fury he'd kept in for so long. One glance imprinted the entire crowd on his brain. Jonas' posture showed his sureness, his blocky, angry face and neck wide open. McKee controlled his growing relish for this. He held back his excitement. He nodded, slowly.

'If the hostler finds poison,' he said, 'I'll show you my example.'

He half-turned as if to walk off the porch, deliberately giving Jonas the opportunity to start his fight. The huge man grabbed at McKee's arm to whirl him around.

McKee side-stepped, completed his turn,

jerking his sleeve free of the outstretched fingers. Thrown off balance, Jonas weaved, crouched lower while he regained his footing. He moved in fast, hooked a left at McKee's chest and aimed for his jaw with an explosive right.

Both missed. McKee merely kept moving to the left, causing the vicious right to slash past his shoulder. Pulled more off balance, Jonas began to straighten and weave back toward his prey.

McKee struck out with his open right hand, slamming the heel solidly into Jonas' throat. The blow stopped the huge man where he stood. He let out a choking scream and rocked back on his feet. He grabbed desperately at his throat to squeeze air into his lungs.

McKee could have let him fall, but a simple victory wasn't enough to appease his wild destructive rage. His right arm shot out and his fingers closed on the lapels of Jonas' broadcloth. He kept the giant upright, smashed his left into Jonas' face once, again, and again. He wanted to punish, to hurt and destroy this cause of his family's fear, to repay with a fierce savageness the terrifying emptiness he'd felt while he held Maryann's tiny fingers and stared down at the pitiful convulsing dog. His right hand twisted the coatfront tighter. Jonas' knees began to buckle. McKee drove his fist in harder. Jonas' nose flattened with a sickening crunch.

A hand grabbed McKee's shoulder, pulled at him. 'That's enough! Stop it!' Royce's voice called, 'That's enough, Ben!'

McKee's grip slackened. Jonas dropped like a heavy sack to the porch floor, gasping for breath, blood pouring from his nose. His legs thrashed as he fought to draw air into his body.

Haycox was beside Royce. 'Take him in,' the rancher said. 'He almost killed that man. You take him in.'

'What do you mean?' Hy Loomis cried from the street. 'He started it. He went after Ben.' Muttering, then talk broke out. 'Yeah,' another man yelled. 'Ben had a right to defend himself.'

Royce said, 'Get out of here, McKee.' He saw that Haycox was going to speak up and he added, 'You've had all the trouble you're going to have. Once more, I'll lock you up 'til Mr Basso leaves. You keep clear of him.'

McKee nodded, then started at Basso. The cattle buyer's black eyes were tight, his forehead deeply wrinkled. He seemed puzzled, his chest rising and falling rapidly as he looked down at the prostrate giant. McKee began to turn. At once Basso raised his head. The narrowed eyes and hard mouth gave Basso's face an expression McKee had seen once before in a New Mexico courtroom.

'He'd better keep clear,' Basso said. 'I've had enough of him. From now on my men will wear their guns.'

99

McKee, cautious and tense, said nothing. Charlotte and the children waited in the darkening street beyond the porch. He started off the steps.

Basso stepped close to Jonas, on his knees now, massaging his neck with both hands. A tinge of whiteness, sallow under Basso's tan, showed on both of his cheekbones. One corner of his mouth twitched. His glare raked the onlookers, stopped on Cooley's whiskered face.

'Take Jonas to the doctor's,' he said. 'While he's being patched up, you get back to the hotel. I want protection against that storekeeper.'

Then he brushed past Haycox and walked from the porch.

CHAPTER TEN

'Wowie!' Tommy cried. 'Boy, Dad, you sure gave it to him!' He skipped joyfully a few steps ahead of his father and turned to Fred. 'You see him do it, Freddy? You see him?'

'Yuh. Boy oh boy!' He grinned up at Loomis. 'That'll teach them to stay away from us, won't it, Mr Loomis?'

'Come on, kids,' McKee said. 'Hurry up. Keep ahead of us.'

He watched them a bit grimly as he walked.

They were like new people now, their depression completely gone. For the first time since Tommy was given the derringer, they were the happy children he'd cared for and watched out for and loved from the moment of birth. The defeat of Jonas meant freedom to them, but his family was not free, and McKee knew it. He had brought the problem out in front of the townspeople, yet he actually hadn't settled a thing. He'd only given Charlotte and the children a reprieve which would be no longer than Basso allowed it to be.

He glanced back through the gathering darkness. Many of the families had left the town hall. Two farmers' wagons headed out of town. The hotel porch lamp had been lighted, and he could see Basso going into the lobby. Cooley walked with Jonas toward the doctor's office.

Tommy and Fred ran up their front walk. Charlotte fingered into her dress pocket for the key. When she had the door open, McKee put Maryann into her arms. 'I'll be up in a few minutes,' he told her. 'I want to talk to Hy.'

'Don't stay out, Ben. Please.'

'I'll be in. Get the kids settled.'

He waited until the front door closed, then again turned back to the street. The valley night came fast. Over the circle of mountains stars winked and multiplied. While the sky blackened long squares of yellowish light streamed down into Main as lamps went on in a few of the houses. Every first-floor window and door of the town hall was brightly illuminated. The shadowy forms of the adults who'd remained for the dance moved back and forth inside.

McKee said to Loomis, 'I won't go to the store until Basso leaves. You handle it. If he causes any trouble in there close up. I don't want you giving them any reason to go after you.'

'Let me stay here with you. I could use the couch downstairs. I'd hear if anyone tried to get in.'

In the darkness McKee could not distinctly see the expression on the clerk's fat face, but he knew the feeling that was there. 'Stay clear of this house from now on, Hy. No matter what happens, keep out of it.'

'They'll come, Ben. Basso looked crazy after you licked his man. You should get out of town. You can't keep Charlotte and the kids locked up in there.'

'Where can we go? Basso and his men can cover this valley in a morning.'

'Someone could hide you. I could help by ridin' out...'

'No. You'll help more if you stay away and keep the store going. Watch for Cooley and Jonas. They're still in Doc Ward's.'

McKee remained on the steps, watching until Loomis was safely past the town hall. The moon topped Elbert Peak, full and bright,

102

promising one of those clear, white-blue nights so typical of the high country. He stared intently at the windows on the second floor of the hotel. Basso's room would be the lighted middle one. A mosquito played near McKee's ear and he brushed it away. As far as he could see, the window shade was drawn. Behind the shade he knew Basso was waiting, planning.

The door of Doctor Ward's house opened and Cooley stepped out. The tall whiskered man crossed Main toward the hotel.

McKee slapped at the mosquito, turned, opened the door and went into his house.

* * *

Basso stood with the wall lamp to his back, staring out past the edge of the shade. He'd noted the moonlight had supplanted the first darkening of night. Cooley, on the porch steps, was almost daylight plain to him. The moon, even the illumination thrown by the stars, was something to be used, figured in; plans, to Basso, were always subject to change. Jonas' defeat had been a surprise. He hadn't realized the full extent of McKee's explosive fury. The hateful, uncontrollable anger he'd felt outside had left him as he'd stood here with his eyes on the street. What the people had seen would work more for him than McKee. The clear vision the moon gave would help. He'd use the stars, the weather, anything to repay McKee.

103

Somewhere in one of the other rooms a clock chimed the hour. Giles Basso listened, counting.

'Seven,' he muttered. He smiled to himself. 'We've got the whole night.'

He turned while he spoke and walked to the hall door. He was calm. He was always calm. He prided himself on that fact. Now he did ... He could never forget the one minute he'd lost his control eighteen years ago. His two sons had died. He'd lain there with the white-hot pain knifing through his side, looking at his dead boys, and he'd tried to get away. Now, he had the man who'd run past his sons' bodies as if they were only potato sacks lying there. He had McKee cornered in this basin. He'd taken whatever they'd given him to do in prison. He'd done every job, accepted every humiliation calmly ... and he'd gotten out five years early. Model prisoner, they'd called him. He was calm while he waited to hear Cooley's footfall in the hall. He'd stay calm.

Once more he reviewed what he'd accomplished since he'd come to Buffalo Hole. From the first Haycox had been sold on his idea of buying the valley's cattle. Oursler had taken longer to convince, but he had Oursler in town now. The man was a crank, distrustful of what seemed too good to be true. He'd left Oursler alone with the contracts, showing he had nothing to hide. Once Oursler decided, he'd back anything Basso did. Haycox controlled the sheriff. He had no worry in him. But he needed Oursler. Haycox and Oursler together could control the people. No one had interfered while McKee fought Jonas man to man. The McKees still had friends. They'd be shocked at the deaths of the woman and three children...

He visualized the homes adjacent to McKee's, the barns, the spaces between the yards. He mentally saw McKee, his woman and kids in the home, the closeness of the neighbors, the distance a man would have to run to get back to the hotel once a shot was fired. Basso's face was wooden, his eyes tight. The smile returned. He nodded.

Footsteps approached in the hall. Basso turned the knob. Cooley stepped inside. 'Jonas won't be long,' he said. 'The doc started on him soon as we got inside.'

'You told him to come back here?'

Cooley nodded. 'He's worried you'll climb on him for losin'.' He watched Basso, waiting for an answer. Basso said, 'What are you waiting for? I wanted you up here so you could get your gun on.'

Cooley flushed at the sharp words. He went over to the closet and opened the door. Three holstered sixguns hung on their gunbelts from clothes hooks. A stub-barrelled Greener shotgun lay flat on the shelf. He took the gunbelt that held a big, black-handled Starr .44. He buckled the weapon around his waist and thonged it to his right leg. Then he looked again at Basso.

Basso had returned to the window. His back was to Cooley. He said nothing. Cooley's hand brushed at his brown beard, rubbed his chin.

Cooley stared silently like that for another two minutes before he walked to the dresser and picked up a water glass. He opened the top drawer and took out one of the whiskey bottles that had been left over from last night.

'Wait for that,' Basso said from the window. 'I don't want another slip-up.'

Cooley set the bottle down on the dresser. He flared into speech. 'You think I can't handle McKee? I've handled better than him, and you've seen it.'

'I've seen it. I'm depending on it.'

Cooley placed the glass beside the bottle. Basso dropped the shade into place and said, 'People won't miss Jonas. That bandage makes him stand out, even from here.'

'Don't climb on him,' Cooley snorted. 'You said to let McKee get in a couple good punches before he gave it to him. You should've had Jonas open up right off. Dammit, I don't go for this push-pushin'. I'm not wearin' this belt to spend my time givin' kids guns and breakin' horses' legs.'

Giles Basso studied Cooley with calm speculation and liked what he saw. Watching Jonas take a beating had keyed up Cooley. He was on edge, prepared for anything. Cooley

106

was a man of action, not talk, but he was a thinker, too. He knew with the instinct of a gunfighter when he was ready to go after a man. He was ready now. All he needed was the word.

'Did you see Haycox out there?' Basso asked.

Cooley looked at Basso quizzically. 'He went into the Stockman's buildin'.'

'Fine. That's fine,' said Basso calmly.

Both men turned as the door opened. Jonas Foss came inside. A white bandage covered the entire top half of his nose, but he was so big it seemed small. He halted beside the dresser, took the bottle and poured a double shot into the glass.

'Go ahead,' Basso told him. 'You've earned it.'

Jonas drained his glass. He stared at his gunbelt and the shotgun in the open closet.

'McKee'll come out,' he said flatly. 'I want one more crack at him.'

'Not you, Jonas,' Basso said. 'You'll stay in here. People will expect you'll go after McKee. They'll wait for it. They won't look for Cooley to go down to McKee's house and draw him out.'

Cooley laughed. 'I'll call him so the whole town can hear.'

'No, you'll draw him out. Him or one of his family,' Basso corrected. 'People will be asleep by midnight. You can go around by the flat.

107

You make noise, someone will look out a window. That's all there'll be to it.'

Cooley nodded. 'Okay. I'll go down to the bar now. Let people see me in there.'

Basso shook his head. He stepped to the bureau, took the bottle and poured a drink. 'You'll wait 'til Haycox and Oursler come up. Then you'll go down for more glasses. I want the three of us in this room when they get here.'

'I told you Haycox went into the Stockman's building.'

'He'll come. Both him and Oursler,' Basso said. 'They want that contract I've offered them. We'll wait right in here for them.'

CHAPTER ELEVEN

For the past half-hour Ben McKee had stood at the parlor window. He'd stayed upstairs until the children were in bed. The boys were restless, so Charlotte had remained across the hall in their bedroom sewing until they fell asleep. McKee watched the street and the people who came along the walks. He watched the lamps go on inside the houses and the shadows of movement behind the drawn shades and curtains. He kept his tall body to the edge of the window, giving no one outside a chance to spot where he stood. He'd done all this before. He clearly remembered the long hours he'd spent doing just this same thing in other towns while he'd been a lawman.

That had been so long ago, he'd forgotten what it was like to have his life depend on what he saw. He couldn't afford to miss anything in those days, a stranger's arrival in town, a drunken cowhand who was out for trouble; even the way a man walked or sat his saddle, how a man tied his gun, had told him what to expect. It had taken a lot of years to change him, but he had changed. He was a storekeeper. He thought like a storekeeper. He watched people's eyes to judge their needs, to be ready with an answer if they questioned some food or product he handled. For the last five years he'd rarely thought of his life as a lawman. This minute he was aware of little else. He'd taken on the same watchful habits, felt the same mistrust about each sound he heard. He waited with his nerves continually tense, watching for something to happen.

He did not turn, he simply kept his attention on the street when Charlotte came in from the hallway. She stopped a few feet behind him.

'What will we do, Ben?' she said. 'We can't keep the children locked up inside the house. Basso could stay a month.'

'I know it,' he answered bitterly. 'We can't stay. We can't run. We can't even fight without the whole thing going against us.'

'You won. Even the boys saw that.'

He looked at her. 'They didn't see that the

109

fight gave Jonas and Cooley a reason to carry their guns. It gave that ape enough reason to come right into this house after me.'

'Shhh. Please, darling. Not so loud. They'll hear.'

He waved her silent. 'They'll hear more than that before this is over. Fine head of a family I am. Fine father. I have my one chance to show it is Basso who's after me, and I do exactly what he wanted. The smart, capable lawman, Ben McKee. He goes up to a hotel room wearin' a gun. He thinks the fact he wore a badge once makes him different from other people. Well, he isn't.'

'Please, Ben. Please.'

'Oh, come on. You know I've handled this all wrong. I believed the law would back me. I thought Haycox would have enough faith in me to know after ten years of doing business with me that I wouldn't lie about this. I didn't figure on cattle bein' more important than us. Dammit, I should've gone into that hotel and started shootin'. If I had any guts, I'd take that Winchester and go up there now. I should cut those three down. I should kill them before they can think up one more crazy way of getting at you and the kids.' He gestured with one hand at the carbine on the mantelpiece and added angrily, 'The hell with what happens to me, I'm goin' ...'

Charlotte slapped him hard across the face. The whack of her small open palm was loud in

110

the room. He stared at her, shocked, his eyes watering from the sting. Her stare met his and held. She was not angry or nervous. She was hurt.

'Don't ever say that again,' she said. 'What happens to you means everything. Everything. I'll do that again if you say it.'

'But I can't...'

'Can't think of what to do. That's nothing to be mad at yourself for. You're up against an insane man who's thought out everything you might do. He's clever and he's ruthless, and he has all the strength on his side.'

'I haven't even put up a sensible fight.'

'Going into that hotel with a rifle isn't sensible. Besides, you couldn't just shoot a man. You believe in the law. When I met you, that's all you lived for. It's let you down. But you could no more go against what you believe than you could have refused to fight that brute Jonas.'

He shook his head. 'Charl, I can't keep you and the kids locked up in here. I should have tried to get out while Queen was alive. I should've moved you and the kids to someplace like the rock cabin. There'll come a night when they'll shoot at the shadows behind the shades. I can't ask any of our friends to take us in. Basso will kill ten people if he has to.'

She nodded and pressed her body close to his. She raised her hand and touched the cheek she'd slapped. 'I'm sorry. I need you the way

111

you are, not … you're not mad at me?'

'Roaring mad. I'll think of some way to get even.' He lowered his face and kissed her. Then, suddenly, she began to cry, completely, helplessly, making no sound so the children wouldn't hear. He led her to the horsehair sofa and they sat. He held her tightly. He spoke softly to her, felt her body cease its slight trembling.

They heard the scuffing of a shoe outside on the sand of their front walk. McKee got to his feet quickly. He had the Winchester in his hands by the time someone knocked on the door.

He motioned for Charlotte to stay in the parlor. Then he moved to the hall doorway. 'Who's there?' he asked.

'Oakley Haycox, and Mr Oursler,' said Haycox's voice. 'We want to come in.'

McKee leaned the carbine against the wall and walked into the hallway.

Oakley Haycox stepped into the house first, then Will Oursler and Nate Royce. Haycox's thin leathery face glanced through the doorway to Charlotte.

'I don't want to waste any time,' he began. 'We've just come from talkin' to Basso.'

'Step into the parlor,' said McKee. 'I don't want to wake up the kids.'

Haycox's face hardened but he followed McKee from the hall, his limp more noticeable now that he was irritated. He was going to

112

continue when Oursler spoke up. 'We spent almost an hour talking to Basso,' he said. 'He's about had it with you.'

'I've about had it from him, Mr Oursler.'

Haycox opened his mouth, then shut it when Oursler glanced at him. Oursler was going to handle this, that was clear. He was a tall, long-boned man, possibly five years senior to Haycox. In ten years McKee had seen him in town only eight or nine times, and every time he'd looked the same. He wore a stiff, gray woolen suit that seemed awkward on his body. He was cleanly shaved, his shaggy white hair brushed straight back over his long ears. He, like Haycox, had driven his own herd in to stock the virgin range, but once he had his ranch built, he seldom left it. His foreman did all his buying in town. He wanted nothing, understood nothing except his land and cattle. He was an honest and forthright man, faithful to his word and friends. As he studied McKee's face, his own held no softness or friendship.

'Oakley told you exactly what Basso has offered to do here,' he said.

'I know why Basso's here. I told Oakley Haycox.'

Oursler nodded. 'Oakley came to me with Basso's first letter last June. We're locked up in this Hole half the year, but we're no fools, McKee. Both Oakley and I sent letters out to towns and cattlemen who'd done business with the Basso Company. We checked on the owner, this Giles Basso.' He leaned his long body forward a bit, pounded his left fist into his right hand for emphasis. 'Every single person we wrote to said the same thing. Basso was honest, fair, and he backed up any contract he signed.'

'I arrested that man down in New Mexico, Mr Oursler.'

'He claims he's never seen you before. He's a wealthy man. The money he has with him proves that.'

'He's built up a business. I know that. But he did it with money he said he stole from a bank.' Immediately, McKee regretted he'd made the statement, for Haycox said, 'Hell, Will. I told you how far-fetched this whole thing was. You see? You can't talk to him.'

McKee said, 'That dog dying isn't far-fetched. There was poison on that cookie, and that dog ate it. I say Jonas left that cookie on that chair near my daughter so she'd pick it up.'

Oursler nodded. 'That dog was poisoned. Lerrazza's pretty sure it was arsenic. But he's not sure it was from a cookie. The dog had been begging from everyone in the hall.' Haycox began to interrupt and Oursler turned on him. 'Oakley, you shut up. I'm handling this.' Then Oursler's stare returned to McKee.

'There is something wrong here,' the rancher said. 'There isn't a person in town who isn't worried about it. I'd be a fool if I didn't realize what could've happened in that hall.' He glanced at Royce near the parlor door. Royce's mouth was bitten into a thin line, and his eyes were tight as he listened. 'Nate's going to look into the whole thing. He'll talk to people who were there and see if anyone noticed who put that cookie down. Until he does learn something, I want your word you won't try to push Basso.'

McKee sighed. 'Nate won't learn anything. Jonas was too smart to be seen. What happens then? Basso will still be in town.'

'He won't be after Monday night,' Oursler said. 'We've finished with the contracts. He's leaving on the first stage. If you think there's danger to your family, then you keep them inside this house.'

'That won't protect us,' Charlotte said sharply.

'Mrs McKee, the sheriff's agreed to keep a watch on your house. I think your husband has Basso mixed up with someone else. But if you're worried, the law will give you protection.'

'All night tonight. All tomorrow and Monday. Nate Royce has to eat and sleep. Those men only need ten seconds to shoot one of us through a window.'

'Now, listen, Mrs McKee. I'm trying to help you.'

Ben McKee interrupted. 'All right, Mr Oursler. We'll take that. Nate watches the
115

house to see no one gets in here. You won't see any member of our family outside.'

Oursler nodded.

'One thing,' McKee said. 'The only one who comes near this house is Hy Loomis. He can bring us our food.' He looked at Royce. 'You'll tell him, Nate?'

'What about that carbine?' Haycox asked. 'I don't want...'

'I've got a right to keep that in my house,' said McKee. 'I have a permit. You pass the word to Basso I'll shoot either him or his men if they come near here.'

'That'll be your right,' Oursler said. 'We'll let it go at that.' When Ben nodded, the rancher turned toward the door. Haycox and Royce started out with him.

McKee walked into the hallway. At the door he said to Royce, 'I'm glad Billy didn't come to the box social with us, Nate. He's only eight. He could've picked up that cookie.'

Their stares locked. The veins in Royce's neck seemed to harden. He didn't speak. He followed the two cattlemen outside.

Charlotte was beside McKee when he closed and locked the door. 'Ben, this doesn't settle anything. One of those gunmen could be outside when any one of us passes a window. Basso would burn us out if he had to.'

'Let him burn,' McKee told her. 'We won't be here. We're taking the kids up to the rock cabin for a few days. We can have Hy get a

116

wagon for us. With Nate watching the house, there'll be no way Basso can know we've gone.'

Her face brightened. 'We can do it, Ben. I can get the children's clothes ready before morning.'

'Don't get anything extra ready. Just take what we'll need until Tuesday.' He put his arm around her waist. 'Come on, you've got to have the kids dressed and waiting by the time I get a buggy back here.'

CHAPTER TWELVE

Hy Loomis opened the rear door of his kitchen and Ben McKee stepped inside. Quickly, Loomis shut the door.

'What are you doin', Ben?' Loomis' round face was anxious. 'They catch you out here, they'll kill you.'

'We need your help,' McKee said, and he told Loomis about his plans. 'We'll stay at the cabin until Tuesday to make sure Basso is gone. I need you to get a buggy and horse from Ramon. I'll wait around back until you bring it outside.'

'Sure, Ben. You can wait in here a few minutes. And then follow me. Don't worry about the door. I never lock this house anyway.'

'No. I'll go with you as far as the barn.'

Loomis nodded and walked to the stove to move the coffee pot off the fire. Since his wife had died in 'ninety-two, he'd stayed alone in their house doing his own cooking and cleaning. He took the thick beefsteak he was going to fry from the skillet, laid it on a plate and returned it to the icebox. He went to turn down the wall bracket lamp.

'No, leave the light on,' McKee said. 'If they're watching you, they'll think you're home. Hy, it's got to look as if we're hiding in our house. Nate Royce will be watching, so there won't be any danger to you. I want you to make it look as if you're taking food to us. While you're inside tomorrow night, light the kitchen lamp. There's enough oil in it for about two hours. Monday night do the same thing with the hall lamp. When they're burned out, it'll just look like we've gone to bed.'

'Don't worry, Ben. Basso won't get any idea you're not there.'

They left by the kitchen door. Once outside they hurried along the back side of the houses and stores. McKee slowed before they reached the livery's rear entrance, letting Loomis go in alone. He moved to the tall, thin outhouse, then stood in the building's black shadow while he waited. The full moon was high over the mountain peaks, its whitish floodlight overpowering the countless stars. After the day's heat, the night was chilly, almost damp. He thought of Maryann's croup and he

118

frowned. He knew the cabin would have wood for the fireplace, for he'd cut some himself when the family had been there two weeks ago. They'd simply have to trust that anyone who'd used the cabin since then would have cut more firewood.

He hardly heard Loomis lead the horse and buggy from the livery stable. Loomis held the black gelding to a slow walk so the vehicle wouldn't creak or rumble if the wheels struck a bump or stone.

Loomis handed the reins to McKee. 'I told Ramon I was goin' to make some deliveries in the mornin'.'

'Thanks, Hy.' He turned toward the west end of town.

'Ramon says he saw those two men of Basso's in the Frontier,' Loomis said. 'Wait a few minutes. I'll go down and check. If I stay inside, it means they're still in there.'

'Don't you stick your neck out.'

Loomis chuckled. 'Don't worry, Ben. I've got a private belief that all us fat men are cowards. We're too heavy to take chances on havin' to run.'

Loomis retraced his steps back to his house. He went in through the kitchen and put out the lamp before he left by the front door. The music of 'Turkey-in-the-Straw' was loud in front of the town hall. Loomis walked past without looking at the men and women who'd come onto the porch between dances. He

119

didn't want to get into a conversation or do anything that could hold him up.

Loomis was worried and afraid. He could see Nate Royce stood in the street opposite the McKee home, but it was the rear of the house that bothered him. If Basso had one of his men spotted back there...

It was more than just the fact he worked for McKee. Ben was his friend. Ben's wife and children were, in a way, the family he'd never had. The loss he had felt when his wife died, the emotional period he'd gone through after that, had been helped by Charlotte and Ben. Charlotte had prepared meals for him, and she'd had him in for dinner. They'd included him when they had friends over for an evening. Hy was Maryann's godfather. He felt more like a grandfather to the kids, the way they came to him and played with him. His concern for them increased as he stepped onto the saloon porch. Then, when he saw that Cooley and Jonas both were inside, he forced his paunchy body to appear relaxed.

Cooley stood against the far end of the smoke-filled bar, his back to the wall. Beside him Jonas leaned with his legs spread wide while he downed a shot of whiskey. Both men momentarily ceased their talk to glance sideways at Loomis. Loomis worked along the bar, speaking to a few of the men lined there, nodding to others. He stopped opposite the long backbar mirror.

120

The bartender, a round-shouldered, take-your-time kind of man with thin gray hair combed to cover a bald spot, slid a glass under Loomis' nose and asked, 'Say when, Hy.'

'Three fingers,' Loomis said. 'How're you, Mal?'

'Fair. Fair enough.' He poured the drink. 'Havin' another? I'll leave the bottle.'

'You better. The way Ben's got himself locked up, I won't be goin' down to his house tonight.'

He lifted his glass and sipped his drink. He'd spoken loudly enough for Cooley and Jonas to hear. He drew a wrinkled perfecto and struck a match, watching Basso's men above the bright flame. They had heard, he knew.

Loomis stayed at the bar until eleven-thirty. He talked to one town man or another, keeping his conversation casual. Cooley and Jonas remained at their end of the bar. They acted just as casual, were friendly to any of the town men who spoke to them. The square dance was over, and the last of the farmers' wagons were rolling noisily out of town by the time Loomis paid for his bottle and left.

He felt light-headed, realized he was going to have a hangover in the morning. But he was happy and satisfied. His presence in the bar had held Basso's men there, especially after he'd made the remark about the McKees. He'd given Ben three good hours to get well clear of town.

The moment Loomis went past the saloon window, Jonas set down his glass. He started to move up the bar.

Cooley touched the huge man's hand. 'Hold it. Don't make it look like we're followin' him.'

Jonas stopped, returned his boot to the brass rail. He poured another drink. They waited another five minutes. Then Cooley said quietly, 'Okay. If the hotel clerk's waitin', you keep him busy.'

Cooley dropped a twenty-dollar bill on the bar. 'Thanks, Mal,' he said. 'Keep the change.'

The bartender picked up the money. 'Sure thing ... say, thanks, Mr Cooley, Mr Foss. Thanks a lot.' He watched the two men open the door and step into the hotel lobby.

Tetterman sat behind the registration desk, bent over some paper work. He'd looked up when he heard the saloon door open.

'Good evening. Good evening,' he said pleasantly. 'I've waited here all night. No one's gone up to Mr Basso's room since Oursler and Haycox left.'

Cooley nodded. He continued on to the staircase, while Jonas stepped to the desk. 'Mr Basso wants us to pick up his ten thousand dollars,' Jonas said. 'I'll take it now.'

'Of course,' the hotelman answered. He glanced toward the stairs as he came around the counter.

'Cooley will cover me from the room,' Jonas explained. He followed Tetterman into his office and shut the door behind him.

Tetterman kneeled at the iron safe behind his desk. 'You tell Mr Basso I'll be happy to keep anything he wants in here,' he said while he worked the lock.

'I will,' Jonas told him. 'You've certainly been a big help to him, Mr Tetterman. We certainly appreciate it.'

*   *   *

Cooley made his way cautiously alongside the barn behind the McKee house. He'd run all the distance from the hotel, but he'd been careful to conserve his breath. He didn't know how fast his chance would come back here. He wanted to be prepared if it came right away. Not being careful enough had been Jonas Foss' mistake. Cooley knew himself to be a smarter, better man than Jonas, but he did not underestimate McKee. He was going to shoot the first person he saw inside the house, no matter who it was. He'd need his breath to get back to the hotel before one of the neighbors spotted him.

A buggy rumbled past out on Main as he turned the corner of the barn. He could hear the driver call something to Sheriff Royce.

Cooley smiled. Basso had dropped the idea of asking McKee to stay inside his house to

123

Oursler and Haycox. That knack of split-second planning every action right down to the smallest detail was what kept Cooley working for Basso. He'd even been right about the moon. It was lower toward the southwest, behind the peak of the house's roof. The deep shadow of the building was all the cover Cooley needed.

Another wagon rolled by out in the street. Cooley drew his Starr revolver, bent over and grabbed a handful of dirt.

He threw the dirt against the kitchen door. The noise of the gravel and small pebbles hitting and falling was loud. He wasn't sure the sheriff hadn't heard.

He slid along the rear of the house and looked beyond the lawn to the street.

Royce stood on the opposite walk. He hadn't changed his position.

Quickly, Cooley felt around the ground for small stones. When he'd found six of them, he moved to the middle of the yard.

He threw two stones underhand up against the window of McKee's bedroom.

The stones hit the glass with sharp pings and fell in the dust. Cooley crouched, his sixgun held up, ready.

Nothing happened.

Cooley tossed the rest of the hard stones against the window pane. There was no sound or movement within the house. Cooley, still bent low, searched the sand for a rock. He found one about half the size of his doubled fist.

A wagon came along Main from the direction of the town hall. Cooley waited. The instant the creaking, rumbling noise of the vehicle was opposite the house, he threw the rock through the bedroom window.

Glass shattered, fell to the dust below the window. The absolute absence of any sound or movement was enough for Cooley. He holstered his .44, then ran back alongside the barn.

The lobby was empty when he opened the hotel's rear door. The tiny night lamp which had been left burning threw its light only near the registration desk. Cooley moved hurriedly up the staircase to the second floor.

Basso listened in silence to what Cooley had to report. 'That damn fat storeclerk,' Cooley said when he'd finished. 'He knew McKee was gone from that house. That's why he stayed in the saloon so long.'

Jonas Foss shifted his weight. 'I'll handle him, Mr Basso. Five minutes, and I'll find out where they went.'

Giles Basso rose and stretched his arms. He looked sleepy. 'Don't go near the clerk,' he told them. 'We'll find where McKee took his family.'

'Mr Basso, give me a chance. I muffed that fight. I won't make any more mistakes.'

'I don't figure you will. Not if you want to

keep working for me.' Basso began to undo his tie. He added more casually, 'McKee couldn't move his whole family out without a wagon of some kind. There will be tracks in the morning.' He turned to Cooley. 'Haycox wanted to let us take horses to look over the valley. You'll go out and collect them for us.'

Cooley grinned. 'It's dark downstairs now.'

'No. Wait until daybreak. Now, gentlemen, I think we'd better get some sleep before we go out and finish what we've come here for.'

CHAPTER THIRTEEN

Ben McKee did not feel like sleeping. He stood in the cabin doorway listening to the silence of the night. The moon, so bright through the early evening, had slipped behind the southern peaks, making the flat that stretched out on three sides seem like a black, still sea. He could hear only the muted gurgle of water over the sandy bottom of the mountain stream that ran beside the cabin. The single sign of movement was the flickering phosphorous gleam of fireflies among the cottonwoods and willows along the water's edge.

Charlotte came up behind him in the darkness. 'They're all asleep,' she said. 'You should get some rest, Ben.'

'In a little while. You go ahead.'

She touched his cheek with a kiss. He leaned the Winchester against the doorjamb and put his arm around her. 'It's so quiet,' she said. 'I just want Tuesday to get here so I can feel this quiet at home again.'

'Don't think about it.'

'I can't help it. This is the first time I've been relaxed since Basso stopped at our house.'

'Stay that way for the kids. They'll forget fast if we act natural.' He kissed her forehead and she went back to the children.

He picked up the carbine again. He had a feeling of safety, but he couldn't be certain they were safe. His reactions were so much different than they'd been while he was a lawman. He'd faced trouble as it happened, confident in his ability to think and act and use a gun. It was so different with Charlotte and the children to think of. What he felt was worry, always worry that couldn't emotionally or intelligently be pushed from his mind.

He'd taken every precaution he could think of coming down to this southwestern end of the Hole. The rock cabin had been constructed as a home by a settler named Walter Abrahamson. After Abrahamson built a farm out on the flat, he'd allowed the cabin to be used as a camping place for town families. For the last four summers the McKees had taken their turn for a two-week vacation with the Gilmartins and other friends of the Abrahamsons'. Tonight McKee had driven the buggy east along the

127

road so it would look as if he'd headed for the pass. He'd turned off on a farm road where his wheel tracks wouldn't show. Then, at the eastern foothills, he'd cut back across the plain. Here the broad grass flat ended and the country tipped up close to the rim. He'd kept to the rocky land, skirting the number of dry washes that cut through at various angles. Cedars grew on the slopes above the cabin. He'd hidden the horse and buggy there.

He closed the door, walked to the fireplace and put another log on the fire. He stepped over to the small crib they kept here for Maryann. The baby breathed easily, with no trace of croup. The cabin was scantily furnished: four bunks next to the stone walls, six rawhide bottom chairs, shelves built like a bookcase beside the door, a table. McKee moved one of the table chairs close to the window. He laid the Winchester across his lap and tried to doze off.

* * *

'C'mon, Dad. Get up. It's almost eight o'clock.'

McKee opened his eyes and straightened in the chair. Fred stood beside him, tucking his shirt into his pants. Charlotte was at the fireplace. Fully dressed, she'd already started breakfast. The rich good smell of bacon and eggs were strong in the room.

McKee stood, glanced at Tommy who hurriedly tried to tie his shoelace. Maryann lay in her crib playing with her rag doll. McKee stretched, then rubbed at the stiffened muscles in his back.

'Why didn't you wake me up?' he said to Charlotte.

'You were sleeping so peacefully,' she answered.

'Hey, can we go out 'til breakfast?' Fred asked. 'Come on, let us, Dad?'

McKee looked at Charlotte. She frowned, her pretty face lined for a moment. The concern was still there when her eyes met Ben's.

'We'll need water,' McKee said to the boys. 'You get it. No fooling now. Stay close to the cabin.'

'We sure will,' Tommy cried. He was out the door a step behind his older brother.

McKee walked outside to the woodpile. In the glare of the morning sunshine the flat was calm and peaceful. Two spirals of smoke twisted skyward from distant farmhouses. Tommy and Fred were joking while they carried the water bucket between them. McKee straightened with a load of wood in his arms, thinking how good it was to hear their talk and laughter again.

He was at the cabin door when the laughter suddenly ceased. The boys ran up behind him. They didn't yell but their excitement showed on their faces.

'There's a man comin',' Fred said. 'A rider,' Tommy added. 'We saw him, Pop, way out on the flat.'

'Get inside,' McKee said. He dropped the wood near the fireplace, then stepped back to the doorway to get the Winchester.

Charlotte started after him. 'What is it, Ben?'

'Stay inside,' he told her. He levered a cartridge into the carbine's chamber and moved through the doorway into the sunlight.

The rider came ahead slowly. He was too far out for McKee to recognize. McKee stepped away from the cabin, putting himself in the open. He had no illusions about the danger of doing this. There were three men after his family. If two closed in on them from other directions, he wanted to know.

The horseman waved his right arm when he was still a half-mile away. He kicked the white stallion he rode, and the animal moved faster.

McKee let the carbine's barrel drop toward the earth. 'It's Walt Abrahamson,' he called over his shoulder. 'It's all right, Charl.'

Relief made McKee's stomach weak. He felt like laughing, but he kept his face serious as the cabin door opened and Charlotte and the boys came outside.

Abrahamson waved again at about a hundred yards distance. He was a heavily built man with straw-colored hair who always smelled of hay and Bull Durham pipe tobacco.

130

He wore farmer's overalls and a faded gray workshirt that bulged out in front under his thick suspenders. He'd lived in Kentucky until his four children were old enough to travel, and then his itch to live in the mountains had brought him to Buffalo Hole. He'd been here sixteen of his fifty-eight years. His three daughters and son had married into local families, keeping the tightly knit relationships they'd always had with Walt and Nellie Abrahamson. His wide, firm mouth broke into a grin when he recognized McKee.

McKee met the farmer as the horse came into the cottonwoods along the stream bed.

'Ben,' Abrahamson said while he dismounted. 'Glad to see it's you.' He smiled at the welcoming yells of the boys and held out his hand. 'I saw the chimney smoke, but I didn't think anyone was goin' to be up here this week end.'

'You don't mind, do you?' Charlotte said. 'We'd like to stay until Tuesday.'

'Stay. Sure, you stay.' His eyes rested on the Winchester in McKee's hand. 'Me and my missus didn't go up for the social. Oliver and Tricia were there. They stopped by last night. That why you're out here, Ben?'

McKee nodded. 'I thought we'd be safer. We made it look like we're staying in our house until after Basso leaves. I'm afraid of what he could do.'

'I don't blame you.' Abrahamson looked at

131

the boys, then from the cabin to the sparse timber along the water. 'Poison...' he said thoughtfully. He shook his head. 'You're not safe here, Ben. I saw your smoke from my place. If anyone does come huntin' you, it wouldn't take them long.'

'We've got more of a chance here. In town they would've been bound to get one of us. I couldn't've made it through the pass. I didn't mean to make trouble for...'

'No. No, that's not it. I was thinkin' it would be safer for you at our place.'

McKee said quickly. 'We can't. You didn't see this Basso. He's not right, Walt. He wouldn't stop with us if anyone helped.'

'That Basso's crazy,' Fred cut in. 'He tried to kill me. He killed our horse.'

'Fred...' McKee said sharply. The boy silenced and McKee turned to Charlotte. 'Take them inside. Their breakfast'll get cold.'

'Come on, boys,' she said. And to Abrahamson, 'We've got plenty, Walter. Come on in.'

'I just might,' the farmer answered, patting his ample stomach. He was smiling. Then, when Charlotte moved with the children toward the cabin, the smile faded. 'Ben,' he went on, 'I figured it'd be you out here. Oliver left town right after that fight you had. He wanted to help you, but there was nothin' he or any of the other farmers could do. Haycox and Oursler buy our hay.' He glanced at the stone building again. 'Everyone knows your family takes its vacation down here. That Basso learns you're not in your house, you'll be cornered in there. It won't be pretty, Ben.'

'I don't want you getting caught in this, Walt.'

Abrahamson's broad face became stubborn. 'My fields caught fire five years ago, remember. My barn went up, too. A storekeeper named Ben McKee carried me on his books for three years 'til I could pay.'

McKee glanced around at the cabin, studied it and the trees which lined the ridge slopes and stream. Slowly he nodded.

'You better have a good appetite,' he said. 'Charl demands an empty plate at her table.'

The farmer laughed and followed McKee into the cabin. Once through the door, McKee leaned the Winchester near the window. Charlotte looked up from the plate she was filling with bacon and eggs.

'Walt wants a man-size helping,' McKee said to her. 'After, we're going to go down to his house with him.'

The Abrahamson farm was two miles north of the stone cabin. Abrahamson had constructed an eight-room, two-floor house alongside Hatchet Creek. He'd built this close to the water because he wanted the shade of the thick timber which lined the banks. The ground was thin and sandy in spots on this east bank, but he liked the flat land and the high

133

sky, and he and Nellie could sit on their front porch after a long day's work and watch the sun lower over the mountains beyond his hayfields. He had ten head of cattle that the McKees passed as their buggy rolled into the farmyard. Nellie Abrahamson, who'd been doing her housework in the living room, stepped out onto the porch. She was a tall, handsome, and generously padded woman with graying hair that she kept tied into a bun at the nape of her neck.

She welcomed the McKees, then nodded her head in vigorous agreement when her husband told her why he'd asked them to come with him.

'Oh, I'm so happy you did come,' she said. 'It'll be so good to have someone in the children's rooms. You won't have to leave Tuesday if you don't want to. Stay as long as you want. You'll really be safe here.'

* * *

Eight miles northeast of the Abrahamson farm Giles Basso jerked the pinto horse he rode to a stop. He cursed wildly, dismounted and walked along the wagon-rutted road, his eyes searching every inch of dirt. Beyond him, Oursler Pass rose into the mountains, but Basso didn't even glance that way.

Cooley and Jonas reined in beside Basso's pinto. 'Cooley and I can go through the pass

134

while you go back to town,' Jonas offered. 'If people see you...'

Basso turned on him, swearing obscenely. 'Shut up. You stupid bungler. That's exactly what McKee wants us to think, that he tried to get through the pass.' Jonas flushed, but before he could answer, Basso added, 'We'll split up. Cooley and I'll take the north side where most of the farms are. You'll go south. Find them! Don't you two talk! I just want you to find where McKee and his family went!'

CHAPTER FOURTEEN

Nellie Abrahamson was an excellent cook. She hastily got together a dinner of fried chicken, corn, fried potatoes, topped off with apple pie that the McKees pitched into with relish. The children played in the living room most of the morning, and Tommy said the farmhouse smelled like Thanksgiving. There was much laughter around the table. The children seemed completely at home and relaxed with the Abrahamsons. It was all very satisfying to Ben McKee, yet he noticed how stiff Charlotte's smiles were, how easily they faded. He felt the same kind of edge no matter how things went. He couldn't throw off that anticipation of what could come. He couldn't help watching for it.

Charlotte remained in the kitchen to help

135

Nellie with the dishes. She put Maryann on the couch for a nap while Ben and Walt took the boys out onto the back porch. Ben sat in one of the pine rockers smoking a cigar with Walt, and they talked about cows and hay with the lazy, easy slowness of well-fed men. Fred and Tommy played on the Abrahamson's homemade checker board. The early afternoon was quiet and warm, with not even a trace of cloud in the high brassy sky. A slight breeze came off Hatchet Creek behind the barn, rustling the curtains and giving the house a comfortable, old-shoe feeling.

Fred stood after he'd beaten Tommy in the third game. He said to Walt, 'Mr Abrahamson, have you seen any flat rocks around here? A couple feet long?'

Abrahamson puffed on his cigar. 'I suppose there could be some along the river.'

The boy stared at his father. 'Can we look, Dad? It'll be just what we need for Queen's grave.'

'Well … yes,' McKee said. He heard the kitchen screen door creak open behind him, then close. Charlotte, her face flushed from the warm kitchen, stepped out. She held Maryann by the hand.

'This little lady isn't going to sleep,' she said in the small gap of silence. 'I thought I'd try to rock her.'

'Mommy, no,' the baby whined. 'I want to play.' She squatted at the checker board and

136

started to pick the checkers off the red and black squares.

Tommy said, 'Can we play in the yard, Pop? We been inside all day.'

'If we're going out to look for a flat stone, I think you'd better stay here and let your meals settle.'

'Aw heck, Dad.'

Abrahamson pushed his heavy-set body out of his rocker. He brushed one workworn hand through his hair. 'I have to get some hay down for the horses. You boys can give me a hand in the barn.' He glanced at McKee, who nodded.

Abrahamson started across the yard with Fred and Tommy. Immediately Maryann ran after them.

'No. No, Maryann,' Charlotte said. She took a step off the porch. Abrahamson swung around and, bending, caught the running child in his arms. 'I'll watch her, Charlotte. You set now.'

Charlotte nodded and she moved back beside McKee. Her stare followed her children and the farmer. She did not speak until they were inside the barn. 'I wish it was next Tuesday,' she said flatly. 'Or next Friday.'

'It will be, dear.' He touched her hand but she pulled away. Then, realizing what she'd done, she took his hand in hers.

'I can't stop worrying, Ben. I can't help it.'

'Don't, honey. Walt will watch them every minute. And Nellie, too.'

Laughter came from the barn, the shrilling of the boys' voices merging with the neighs of a horse. In the quiet neither Charlotte nor Ben spoke while they listened to the happy sounds of their children. Maryann appeared in the open barn doorway. 'Mommy,' she called. 'Come see horsie. Come see horsie, Mommy.' The baby started out into the yard.

'Don't come out, Maryann. Stay there,' Charlotte said. 'Mommy'll go.' She stepped hurriedly off the porch into the sunlight, with Ben a stride behind her.

The shot came in that instant, a sharp crack of noise exploding across the flat. Charlotte was thrown to the right as though she'd been shoved aside by a giant hand. Ben tried to grab her, but she fell too fast, landing face up. Her mouth was open in surprise, her face twisted in an expression of shock that jolted hard and deep into his heart.

He was beside her, seeing the blood reddening the top left shoulder of her white blouse. The rifle banged again from the trees lining the river west of the barn. The bullet nicked the top of his left ear. He sprawled flat, both arms reaching for his wife as he felt his own blood on the side of his face and neck.

*   *   *

'Ben ... Ben...' Charlotte moaned. He said, 'Lie quiet. Quiet.' Across the yard Maryann,

138

dumbfounded by what had happened, still stood between the open barn doors. Abrahamson had dashed from the shadowy interior to the baby's side. 'Keep her in there,' McKee yelled. 'Keep the kids inside!'

Abrahamson picked up the child, then started to pull the closest door shut.

McKee's fingers undid the two top buttons of Charlotte's blouse. He grabbed her right hand, slid it in under the collar. 'Press where it's bleedin', between there and your heart.'

Another shot cracked from the river. The steel slug zinged past, inches above McKee's head, and whacked loudly into a porch post.

'Stay low,' McKee told her. 'There's only one of them, I think. The way he's in the trees he can't hit you again as long as you stay low.' Charlotte nodded, and he looked back toward the house. 'Nellie, Nellie,' he called. 'Throw out my carbine. It's beside the kitchen door.'

A bullet banged, another. Both slugs smashed solidly into the house. McKee had the bushwhacker's position spotted in the thick willows where the creek swung south. The screen door's hinges creaked.

'Throw it on the ground,' McKee said. 'I'll get it.'

The weapon sailed through the air, struck the bottom porch step, and landed in the dust ten feet from McKee. 'Just stay low,' he reminded Charlotte. 'Keep pressin' the wound.'

'I'm all right,' she whispered. 'Your ear...'

'It's okay. Just lay still.' He wiped the blood from his hand onto his shirt and began to crawl for the Winchester.

'Nellie,' he yelled into the house. 'Soon as I flush him, get Charl inside. Inside!'

'Yes, yes, Ben!'

The rifle in the woods fired while McKee pushed himself up onto his knees with the Winchester in his hands. The bullet burned past his left arm as he pumped and fired the weapon. He got off two shots, then ran for the cover of the barn.

The bushwhacker fired again when McKee was five feet from the building. He hurled himself for the side, flattened against the solid wood. The bullet ripped into the corner, tore through, splintering out inches above his head.

He hesitated, panting to get his breath. If there were more than one they would have opened up while he ran.

No sound, no hint of movement came from the river while the bushwhacker watched for McKee to show himself. He couldn't be sure from which side McKee would appear. McKee glanced around at Charlotte. She lay sprawled where he'd left her, the blood bright red on her blouse. Cold rage came over him, an icy feeling that made him shiver. He drew in his belly tight, crouched against the rough boards.

'Walt,' he called into the barn. 'I'm going to the river after him. Get the kids into the house

140

when I pin him down.'

He could hear Abrahamson's muffled answer inside.

'Get them to the door. Be ready, Walt.'

Sounds of movement within the barn, then the low grating of the doors pushed open.

McKee edged around the corner firing as he moved, once, twice, three times. He put the steel slugs into the brush within a few feet of each other, probing in search of his hidden attacker.

No answering bullets came while he charged for the cover of a stubby cottonwood twenty yards behind the barn. He fired once more as he threw himself down behind the tree trunk.

He lay flat, eyes glued to the willows. One shake of a branch, a barrel flash, and he had his man pinpointed. The only sound came from behind him, footsteps running, the loud slam of the screen door as it banged shut.

McKee waited. Silence from the river seventy yards away, an easy rifle shot's distance ... The sun burned down, reflected on the water. He watched the thick shadows of the brush, and he smiled grimly against the tree trunk, thinking how quickly a man remembered what experience taught him. You stayed put when you were pinned in the open, you didn't attack or panic from the slightest safe protection. The trick was to wait until you had your chance.

He raised the Winchester inches so the sun

would strike the barrel and give a dull reflection.

A shot cracked in the willows and the bullet smacked solidly into the tree trunk. McKee fired once, and again and again, his aim deliberate now, sure. He was up, moving forward, when he got off a fourth shot.

Loud noise broke out beyond the trees before he was halfway to the willows. A horse, running hard, splashed water, then crashed into and through the brush on the east bank.

McKee kept to the open, trying to get a glimpse of the horse and rider, but the timber blocked his view.

He didn't slow his stride. He moved into the brush and across the river onto the opposite bank. When he stepped from the trees he could see nothing. The bushwhacker had stuck to the timber, would stay within its cover until he could cut across the flat without being recognized.

McKee found the spot where the man had waited. Bootheels had scuffed the sand behind a long, low rock. Two deep digs showed on the stone where McKee's bullets had chipped the rock. No other evidence remained to show a bushwhacker had been here. The man had even picked up his expended cartridge shells.

McKee shook his head, swore beneath his breath, feeling weariness in every bone and nerve of his body. He'd moved too fast once he was sure his family was inside with the

Abrahamsons. If he'd waited a bit longer to draw the man in closer ... He thought of Charlotte and he started to run again, back through the willows toward the house. The heavy Winchester weighed down his arm. He thought of the blood that reddened his wife's blouse, and he felt weak and hollow, like an old weather-dried stump that was rotted inside.

*　　　*　　　*

Charlotte lay on the living-room couch. Nellie Abrahamson bent over her while she bandaged the bullet wound. Walt was in the kitchen with the children. The farmer held a long-barrelled Spencer rifle in his right hand, and the butt of a revolver jutted out of one pants pocket. Fred started to go into the living room when McKee pushed past the screen door. Walt put his hand on the boy's shoulder, held him back.

'Wait 'til your mother's all fixed up,' the farmer said. 'Just a few minutes.'

'I want to see how she is,' Fred said. 'Let me come in, Dad.'

'No. You wait, son. Give Mrs Abrahamson time to do what she has to.'

The boy didn't speak. He just stood beside Walt with a subdued, troubled expression on his face. Tommy waited in silence, his face pale, lips pressed into a small tight line. McKee stepped close to the couch. Nellie had taken off Charlotte's blouse. The white sheet she'd used

143

as cover was spattered with blood, yet no red had seeped through the large square bandage she'd put on the wounded shoulder.

Charlotte looked completely under control, but Ben caught a trembling of her mouth as she spoke. 'It looks worse than it is,' she said. 'Hit the top of my shoulder, but didn't break the bone.'

'She should see the doctor,' Nellie said. Her round face frowned. 'The bullet could've splintered the bone.'

'I can't have any doctor,' said Charlotte. 'He could lead Basso right out here.'

'Basso'll know quick enough,' McKee told her. 'That bushwhacker will go straight to him.'

Nellie dropped a blood-soaked towel into the water basin on the floor and raised the sheet around Charlotte's shoulders. 'She should get some sleep. That was a shock to her system.'

McKee nodded and stepped aside to let Nellie go into the kitchen. Charlotte turned her face away from the door so the children couldn't hear. She barely moved her bloodless lips. 'Now what? Where'll we go? Where is there to hide so Basso can't kill us one at a time?'

'Please, Charl.'

Charlotte swallowed hard. She didn't answer because Walt Abrahamson had come into the room. The heavyset farmer stopped with his back to the kitchen door. He kept his

144

voice low. 'I figure it'll take that bushwhacker two, maybe two and a half hours to bring Basso out here. You can't stay here.'

'I know, Walt,' McKee said. 'I don't blame you for not wanting...'

'I haven't said what I want. I'm giving the facts as I see them. You don't have to convince me you've been tellin' the truth all along. An inch or so lower and we'd be buryin' Charlotte. You stay here much longer, you will be buryin' someone.' He glanced over his shoulder, saw that his wife was keeping the children in the kitchen. 'You can't go back to the cabin. That's out. You'd never get all five of you into town. I think the best thing to do is to move us all to Oliver's house.'

McKee shook his head. Abrahamson didn't give him time to interrupt.

'It's the only way, Ben. Oliver's place is bigger than ours. He doesn't have any trees in close they can use for cover. We stay on the road there'll be no way of Basso trailin' us there.'

'Oliver has a wife.'

'He has a mother and a father, too. We're in this now. Basso won't stop with you. Don't you worry. They'll take us in. And Oliver has some guns in his house. He can go get Everett and Wade, too. We could get so many armed men around his house that Basso wouldn't dare come close.'

McKee gazed down at Charlotte who stared

up at him with a naked plea. Slowly, he nodded. 'We'll move right away, Walt. I'll leave my family with you and Oliver and I'll go...'

'You won't go anywhere,' Charlotte said fervently. Her face was ghastly white, lips shaking. 'You'll stay with us.'

'Charl, we've run as far as we can,' McKee said. 'With Walt and Oliver, you and the kids'll be safe. I can go in and face Basso.'

'No, you can't.'

'I have to. Whatever we do, we're just putting off the fact I'll have to stand up to him eventually. You're all safe now.'

Abrahamson said, 'You won't have to go in alone, Ben. I can get some of the farmers together. We'll go in with you.'

'That wouldn't work. Basso's too smart. He'd back down, but he'd come into the Hole next year. Or next month. Let me have that sixgun you've got, though.'

Abrahamson's head shook. 'Someone should go in with you, Ben.' He drew the revolver, a bone-handled .44 Colt. To McKee it looked as though it hadn't been cleaned or fired in years. He turned the drum, felt that it tended to stick. He slipped it under his belt, noticing how Charlotte watched him. She no longer was emotional but seemed to study him speculatively.

'You're right, Ben,' she said. 'We'd have to face Basso later if this isn't settled now.'

146

'We?'

'It has to be the two of us. We know that Maryann and Fred and Tommy will be safe with Walt.' She pushed herself up on the sofa, eyes shining intently, the sheet slipping down on her fine white shoulders. 'My shoulder won't keep me from traveling. We could go back to the house and make it look like we're all there. Basso would come after us. He'd have to come after us.'

'No, that's insane.'

'It is not insane,' she spat at him. 'What are you going to do, walk up the middle of the street and face three gunmen? That's what's insane.' Her voice quieted. 'We can make a plan. I can be in the house. You can be outside. In the yard. In the barn. All we need to do is to catch one of those three near our house, and we can prove to Royce that Basso is after us.'

McKee watched her face, frowning thoughtfully. He had never felt so close to her in his life. Or loved her so much. He'd believed he'd known himself and he'd known this woman. That he would ever accept an idea like this . . . but this was a time of change. He felt the tension between them, the hope—yet there was a terrible threat to it, a touch of terror.

'I'll be inside, Ben. I'll have your rifle.'

Slowly he nodded. 'If any shooting does start, you'll fire that carbine and keep firing until Royce comes.' She nodded, and he turned to Abrahamson. 'I'll tell Hy Loomis to get out

147

here if things don't go my way. You can bring your farmers into town then.'

'I think I should take some in anyway.'

'My kids are in your hands, Walt. That's enough.' He looked down at Charlotte, sitting with her hands on her knees, her lovely face very calm.

'You rest while we get things ready,' he said. 'We'll drive into Buffalo Hole as soon as we get the kids safe at Oliver's.'

CHAPTER FIFTEEN

Jonas Foss had felt good all afternoon, but now he'd started to change. He'd gone straight to his room the minute he'd gotten back to town. He'd washed and shaved and had put on a clean suit before he went down to the lobby to wait for Basso and Cooley. They hadn't shown up and he'd visited the barber's for a haircut. It felt good to have the sweat and dust off him after the way he'd ridden in from the Abrahamson house. He felt self-satisfied. He'd be able to tell Basso how he'd fixed it so McKee was pinned down in one spot. Basso would forget the beating he'd taken yesterday. But now, as the hazy summer dusk rose over the wide flat, Jonas wasn't so sure. Basso would have to get back soon or it would be too dark to finish the job.

Jonas pushed open the lobby screen door and walked out onto the porch. To the west the sharp redness had softened to a pink flush between the peaks, and the blue of twilight settled into the valley. The only movement on the flat was the cattle in the distance, and Jonas could barely make them out because of the land shadows. He rubbed his big hand along his thick jowls. He cursed to himself and stepped off the porch.

He wanted a drink. His throat ached with craving for a shot of whiskey, but that was out. All he'd need was to have Basso smell liquor on him at a time like this ... A light came on in the restaurant, another showed behind the Frontier's batwings. Most of the houses had lamps burning in their windows. Jonas angled across Main toward the east end of town. If Basso had made a complete circle of the Hole, he'd come in from that direction.

Then Jonas saw the light go on inside McKee's front room. He halted in the center of the street. His right hand dropped to the long bulge of his holstered Colt beneath his coat. He pressed the weapon hard into his thigh

He swung around to retrace his steps toward the hotel porch. He hadn't figured McKee would bring the family back here. The woman had been down, hit bad from the way she hadn't moved ... Alone now, without Basso to do his thinking, Jonas Foss was lost. Carefully, he touched his bandaged nose, then dropped

149

his hand to his side.

He hurried up the porch steps. McKee's coming back could mean he'd push things all the way. McKee would do some checking first. He'd learn about the horse that had been ridden into the livery all lathered up. He'd put two and two together and he'd come out hunting.

Jonas stopped a foot inside the lobby doorway and stood looking out. The bulk of a buggy and wagon swung into the road from the thickening night alongside the McKee house. Jonas moved a foot further into the lobby's shadows and continued to watch.

McKee drove first to the doctor's house. He was inside only a minute before he returned to the buggy and drove west to the livery stable. The doctor had stepped out of his office carrying a black bag. McKee reappeared from the barn and caught up with him. Together they headed toward the east end. McKee glanced up at the second floor windows when he was opposite the hotel.

'Damn McKee, anyway,' Jonas whispered to the lobby's emptiness. 'Damn Basso for not gettin' back.'

Jonas turned and walked through the lobby into the Frontier Saloon. He didn't know what to do. It would be just a matter of time until McKee questioned him about the horse he'd left in the livery. If he did the wrong thing, he'd have to answer to Basso when he got back.

Jonas halted opposite the backbar mirror where he could watch the batwings. 'Whiskey,' he said to the bartender. 'Leave the bottle.'

'Sure, Mr Foss.'

Jonas gripped the glass the bartender set down and tilted the whiskey bottle. He spilled some of the liquor, but he paid no attention to it. He took a long mouthful, swallowing slowly. The whiskey felt warm, good going down.

A man came in through the lobby entrance. Jonas turned with hasty silence. Reflexively, his hand had dropped to the butt of his Colt. He raised the hand when he saw it was Tetterman.

The long-faced hotelman stopped beside Jonas. 'Oakley Haycox sent a boy over from the Stockman's. He'd like to know what time he can expect Mr Basso back.'

Jonas smiled at his drink. He'd forgotten all about Haycox. His smile moved to Tetterman. 'I'll go over and talk to Haycox,' he said.

Tetterman nodded and began to turn. Jonas said, 'Mr Tetterman, there's no hurry.' He waved one big hand at the whiskey bottle. 'You've been pretty decent to us. I'd like to buy you a drink 'fore we leave.'

The hotel owner grinned happily. 'Well, that's very nice,' he said. 'Very nice.' He stepped in beside Jonas and called to the bartender for a glass.

151

Doctor Ward pulled the sheet up over Charlotte's shoulders and then turned from the bed. He was a tall stringy man in his mid-fifties, gray-eyed and nearly bald. He had a long pointed nose, and large hands that had moved deftly and capably while he'd examined and bathed Charlotte's wound. McKee stared over the doctor's shoulder as he back-stepped from the doorway into the hall. Charlotte lay with her eyes closed. She breathed easily, but her face against the pillow was pale enough under her tan to give her a yellowish, sickly look.

'How is she, Doc?'

'She'll come along all right. But she's got to have plenty of rest. I'll stop in tomorrow morning.'

McKee shook his head. 'I thought I was doing the right thing to bring her in. I didn't know it would take so much out of her.'

'You did exactly as you should have, Ben. That wound was beginning to infect. It would've been much worse if you'd let her stay at Abrahamson's.'

The doctor walked down the stairs ahead of McKee. When McKee opened the front door to let him out, the doctor asked, 'Have you reported this to Nate Royce?'

'No. I will, though. Let me report it, Doc.'

'All right, Ben.' The doctor started off the steps. The night was black-dark in this half-hour before moonrise, the street quiet. McKee did not see anyone else outside, but he heard the sound of footsteps. Doctor Ward was speaking to someone at the edge of the street.

Hy Loomis came up the walk. The short fat clerk broke into speech as he stepped inside past McKee. 'You should've told me you were back, Ben. I wouldn't've known if Ramon hadn't stopped me.'

McKee locked the door, then told Loomis about Charlotte. Loomis frowned, gazed worriedly at the staircase. 'There's only one of those three in town,' he said.

'I know. Will you stay with Charl, Hy?' And, when Loomis nodded, 'Don't do anything, though. Just stay up in the hallway with the Winchester. The downstairs doors and windows are all locked. Anyone tries to get in will make a noise. All you do is start shooting so Royce'll come. I'll get back, don't worry.'

'Sure, Ben.'

McKee went up the stairs and into the bedroom. Quietly, he lifted the Winchester from beside the doorway. Charlotte opened her eyes. She smiled weakly and he walked to the bed.

'I don't know what happened,' she said. 'I just started to feel so sick in the buggy.'

'Doc said there was an infection setting in.' He touched her forehead gently with one long finger, brushing a few strands of her blonde hair away from her eye. 'He gave you

153

something to help you sleep.'

'I can feel it. It makes me feel whoozy. Did you tell Nate?'

'I'm going to see him now.' Her face stiffened and he said, 'There's no danger. None of them is in town. The one who shot you must've gone after the others. Walt was right about leaving the kids at Oliver's. You sleep now.'

'All right, dear.' She smiled. Her voice was faraway. 'Whew. The doctor must've given me something powerful.'

'You sleep.' He kissed her quickly and found her lips warm and still and unresponsive.

Downstairs, Hy Loomis took the Winchester. 'You won't find Nate in his office,' he said. 'He was in the restaurant, last I saw him. He knows you were gone. He came to the door with me when I brought some bacon and eggs over this mornin'. He didn't like it, Ben.'

Nodding, McKee said, 'I don't want you leaving the hall. No matter what happens.'

'I won't.' He walked behind McKee to the door. Once McKee was outside, he paused only as long as it took for Hy to turn the key and remove it from the lock.

The town was still dark. The moon hadn't risen beyond the eastern mountains, but the first of its light gave a whitish sheen to the sky behind the peaks. A slight night wind blew off the river. It felt cool and damp as it evaporated the sweat that wet McKee's face and forehead.

154

The street was practically deserted, yet he did not trust it. He kept his coat unbuttoned, his right hand close to the butt of Abrahamson's Colt. He'd cleaned the weapon the best he could, but he didn't trust that, either. The drum didn't revolve just right, and it bothered him. He'd have to be fast and sure. He couldn't depend on a second shot if trouble came. His eyes slid across the lighted windows, probing the blackness that blotted doorways, lay between buildings and under porch roofs.

He had no feeling of excitement, no heightening of nervous tension. He'd experienced both in other days, in other silent streets. Now he felt only a calm numbness. The tension had been grim and strong since he'd had to stop the buggy a mile from town to allow Charlotte to vomit. She'd started to shake ... he'd held her close while he'd driven the rest of the way. They hadn't talked. He couldn't talk to his own wife, he hadn't known what to say ...

The sheriff's office was empty, with just a low-burning lamp on inside. McKee headed for the hotel, glad Royce wasn't there. He wanted no interference in what he intended to do. He went up the porch steps, opened the screen door, and started across the lobby. He buttoned his coat and altered his path when he looked through the Frontier doorway and saw Jonas at the bar with Tetterman.

Two more town men drank beyond the

backbar mirror. Five men were playing poker at a side table under a hanging lamp. The room was filled with cigarette and cigar smoke that shadowed the light, but McKee knew Jonas caught sight of him the moment he stepped through the doorway.

Jonas, his elbows spread wide, occupied a generous expanse of the walnut and brass. The bandage over his nose made the eyes that watched McKee's approach seem deep-set and far apart.

Tetterman turned toward McKee. 'I thought I asked you to stay out of my place,' he said.

McKee said to Jonas, 'You want to talk in here or outside?'

Jonas smiled briefly as he raised his glass to his mouth. He finished the liquor and placed the glass on the bar. 'I got no reason to talk to you.'

'Here or outside?'

The huge man looked at Tetterman. 'Glad we could have a drink together, Mr Tetterman.' He moved away from the brass rail and started past the tables toward the front door. McKee took a step after him. Tetterman set his glass down as if he meant to stop McKee.

'Keep out of this,' McKee said. He brushed past the hotelman and walked from the saloon behind Jonas.

Jonas went off the porch and into the street,

156

headed for the Stockman's building.

McKee's long-legged stride brought him up even with the huge man. 'You were stupid, Jonas,' he said. 'You gave me a reason to come after you when you shot my wife. You either turn toward the jail or draw right here.'

McKee undid the coat button. Jonas glanced at him with a puzzled frown. 'I don't know anything about your wife. Neither does Tetterman. He only knows you tried to push me in the bar and followed me out. I figure that's enough for that sheriff to lock you up once he finds you.'

'All right. I'll face him at the inquest.' They were almost to the two-story wooden building that housed the Stockman's. Tetterman would have his eyes glued on them from the Frontier window, McKee knew. He said quietly, 'Right here, Jonas.'

Jonas didn't slow his pace. 'You won't shoot me in the back,' he said. He stepped up onto the walk and headed for the building's porch steps.

The short lease on McKee's temper snapped. He swung out with his right, struck his doubled fist across the back of Jonas' neck. The impact of the blow knocked the huge man sprawling into the alleyway.

Jonas scrambled to his knees and pushed himself up fast, crouching his wide back against the clapboards of the building. He cursed furiously and reached for his sixgun.

McKee's Colt jumped into his hand. The

157

weapon leveled off directly into Jonas' bandaged face.

Jonas' hand dropped to his side, a strange fear completely claiming him. He stared at McKee, knowing he could die right here.

They were silent another moment, both motionless in the shadowy darkness of the alleyway. Then McKee said, 'You'll tell Royce and Haycox you shot my wife. You'll tell them about Basso and me.'

'Basso'll have me killed.'

'You'll tell them.'

Jonas straightened, kept his back flat against the building. His eyes flicked to the street at the east end of town, then returned to McKee. McKee also had heard the slow clopping of two walking horses. He backed further into the blackness.

Basso and Cooley materialized out of the darkness of the street. They looked as worn out and as tired as the horses they rode.

Jonas said, 'I don't tell anythin'. I face your court, I get a year, maybe two. Cooley ain't all Basso can get. I wouldn't last six months.'

McKee exhaled deeply. He could beat this man, could do anything to him, but Jonas wouldn't talk. If he took him to Royce it would be the same rat race all over again.

He grabbed Jonas' sleeve, jammed the Colt's muzzle into the wide back. 'Down the alley and back toward the west,' he said very quietly. 'Try one thing, Jonas, and I'll kill you.'

CHAPTER SIXTEEN

'They must've come back in durin' the day, Mr Basso. McKee must've figured we'd go out huntin', and he brought them back.'

'All right. All right. Just ride naturally. Don't look around.' Basso's voice was casual, almost indifferent, his relaxed way of sitting his saddle a striking contrast to Cooley's stiffness. 'Damn you, be natural.'

Cooley let his long body slouch. He tightened his knees against his horse's sides to make the animal slow its walk a little.

Watching Cooley, Basso felt his irritation warm to impatience, and he fought to control it. He'd made the mistake when he'd taken Cooley's word that the McKees had run from him. Why hadn't he checked? Why? Basso knew, as he'd learned the hard way, the danger of not checking every last thing that came up. He'd entrusted too much to Cooley and Jonas. He'd be in on everything that happened from now on, wouldn't leave one decision to his underlings ... He'd been tempted to tie his horse outside town when he'd first seen the lamps lit in McKee's home. But he'd held in his anger. The windows close by were too bright. The light thrown by the rising moon was already too damned white, illuminating the sandy lawns and yards too damned clearly.

He looked straight ahead as he spoke. 'To the hotel I'll send for the hostler to get the horses.'

'Right, Boss.'

'Dammit, don't call me "Boss".' He swung his horse to the left slowly. The windows of their rooms on the second floor were dark. There was no sign of Jonas Foss on the walks or porches. A man watched the street from the Frontier batwings, a man too small to be Jonas. Then he recognized who it was. 'Keep quiet,' he ordered. 'I'll talk to Tetterman.'

Tetterman pushed through the batwings before they reached the hitchrails. The hotelman scurried along the walk. His bony face was flushed when he met the horses.

'Mr Basso,' he said. 'I don't know if your man Jonas has had trouble with McKee. He went off with him a few minutes ago.'

'He went off with McKee?'

'Yes.' He took hold of Basso's horse's bridle and held it while he explained. The animal wheeled its stern away from Tetterman as it halted at the hitchrail. 'I couldn't see too well, but it looked to me like McKee pushed him into the alleyway.'

Cooley started to swear, but Basso's words cut him off. 'Will you take our horses to the livery, Mr Tetterman?'

Tetterman nodded vigorously and reached his free hand up for Cooley's bridle. He watched Basso begin to dismount. 'Mr Basso, I

160

think you'd better find out what . . .'

'Now don't get excited. Cooley will go over and see if Jonas went into the Stockman's Club by the wide door.' He gave a small laugh. 'I'm not worried about McKee bothering Jonas.'

As soon as Cooley's boots hit the ground, he started across Main. Basso did not look at Cooley. He stretched tiredly and said, 'You people really have some valley here, Mr Tetterman. I haven't seen finer hay crops in years.' His glance shifted to the western flat, shadowy but clearly visible under the brightening moonlight and starshine. 'I'd say a man would do good to invest money in your future.'

Tetterman grinned widely, on the verge of speaking. Basso added, 'Yes, I'd say more money could be invested here. Mr Tetterman, would you have some water heated for our rooms after you leave the horses?'

'Of course. Right away, Mr Basso.'

Basso went into the lobby, then walked up the stairs to his room. A man came out of one of the other rooms while Basso turned his key in the lock. Basso nodded to the man and said, 'Fine evening,' nodding again to the man's agreement. Basso's face was calm, relaxed, his stance casual. Once he closed the door behind him his features took on an abrupt change.

He swore to himself as he put a match to the wall lamp. He drew in a deep ragged breath and began to walk about in wide aimless circles. He'd believed he'd had McKee, but all he'd done was waste a whole day. He couldn't waste one more minute. He'd told Haycox and Oursler he meant to leave tomorrow. He had to go or they'd see through him. He stopped circling and went quickly to the bottle and glasses on the bureau. He poured himself a glassful of Scotch. The liquor spilled and he wiped it up with his handkerchief. He was careful not to leave one drop of the liquor on the marble top.

He stepped to the window and opened the bottom half to let in air, then he stared out into the wide street. For several seconds he remained motionless, his body slumped forward slightly. Somewhere in one of the close yards a dog barked loudly and a cat screeched. The remote, wild sounds only emphasized the silence of the room. There were the lines of homes with lights bright in their windows, and there was the one house that held the people he'd come to kill, but all around that house were the lights he wanted to put out. Unconsciously, Basso rubbed the thumb and forefinger of his left hand along his chinbone. Suddenly, when he realized what he was doing, he flung the hand away from his face. It was a nervous habit. He couldn't afford to be nervous.

Across Main, Cooley had appeared on the Stockman's building porch with Haycox. Basso moved away from the window. He

162

halted in the center of the room and gulped a long drink of the Scotch.

He finished his drink. Then he poured a basin full of water from the pitcher, took off his coat and tie and rolled up his sleeves.

When Cooley came into the room with Haycox, Basso had his hands and face wet. He turned as Haycox stopped a few feet inside the door. Basso let the soap slide into the basin. He lifted the towel and wiped his face before he spoke.

'What's this about Jonas going to see you?' he asked the rancher.

Haycox looked confused. 'Jonas didn't come to see me. I've been in the Club all afternoon.'

'I looked out back of the Stockman's,' Cooley said. 'Jonas wasn't around anyplace. I don't know what's happened, Mr Basso.'

Basso nodded. He spoke to Cooley very quietly, 'I've had enough of this. Get the sheriff.'

Cooley went out. Basso finished wiping his hands. He threw the towel on the bed.

Haycox said, 'I'm sorry about this, Mr Basso.'

'You should be.' Basso stared bluntly at him, his eyes narrowed and unfriendly. 'I've got more to do than bother with a town that gives me nothing but trouble.'

'This is the last you'll have, I promise you. I'll go out and talk to Will Oursler. We'll...'

'The hell with Oursler. What is he anyway, some kind of a God that you people bow down to? I don't need Oursler. I don't need you to help me. That storekeeper made all this trouble. If he's done anything to my man, I'll go right into his house after him.'

'Listen, Mr Basso...'

'I'm not listening to one more thing you or anyone else has to say.' Basso swung away from the cattleman, walked to the closet and opened the door. He took down the holstered Colt that hung from a clotheshook. He buckled the revolver around his waist, then lifted the double-barreled Greener shotgun from the shelf. Haycox watched silently while Basso broke the weapon to check its breech. Basso kept the shotgun in his hand while he shut the door.

He looked at Haycox. 'Too bad, Haycox. I had some fine plans for this valley.' He leaned the Greener barrel-down against the corner of the bureau and started to put on his tie.

'Mr Basso, we've got a contract,' Haycox said.

'And that contract states either of us can cancel after the first year if we're not mutually satisfied.' He picked up his coat from the bed and put it on. 'All this trouble hasn't made anything satisfactory to me, Haycox.'

Basso stepped to the hall door and opened it. Haycox said, 'This will be settled tonight. I promise. We'll talk...'

'Get it settled, then we'll talk.' Basso stepped into the hallway and moved toward the landing. Haycox trailed along after the cattle buyer, not saying a word.

They were halfway down the staircase when voices sounded out on the porch. Cooley and Sheriff Royce came inside, followed by Tetterman.

'...and it looked like he had a gun under his coat,' Basso heard the hotelman say. 'There was a bulge in front just like when he was in Mr Basso's room.'

Royce was nodding as he met Basso. Basso said, 'Well, what are you going to do, Sheriff?'

Cooley spoke out. 'We looked into the other buildin's. We didn't see nothin' of Jonas.'

'Do you go after McKee or do we?' Basso stared at the lawman with hot furious eyes. 'I want McKee taken in.'

Royce said, 'I'll go down and talk to McKee.'

'I don't want you to talk to him,' Basso snapped in the same dangerous voice. 'I want him taken in.'

Royce pressed the palms of his hands together. 'Mr Basso, I can't arrest McKee unless I have proof he's caused trouble with your man.' He looked at Haycox. 'The people have been talkin' about this. That dog bein' poisoned has got them worried.'

'I'll worry about the people,' Haycox told him. 'They better see what's best for them

165

in this.'

Basso said, 'You decide, Sheriff. I'm going to find out what's happened to Jonas with or without you.'

Royce hesitated, a strained, thoughtful look on his face.

Haycox swore. 'Damn it, Nate. You act, if you know what's good for you.'

Slowly Royce nodded. 'I'll go down and get McKee,' he said.

'We'll all go down,' Basso said irritably. 'I'm not taking any chances on McKee. I'll go right into that house after him if I have to.'

* * *

Ben McKee ran along the backside of the business district. His stride was light, his gaze probing into every patch of moon-thrown blackness. He'd taken too long with Jonas, and he couldn't be certain exactly what Basso would do. Basso would know he had been with Jonas. Tetterman had seen enough to realize what had gone on. The wind seemed colder to him. The moon was like a bright ever-present light, the stars like a thousand cold watching eyes. Basso might be hunting him now. That was why McKee had crossed Main at its western end where the street was darkest.

Jonas wouldn't give him any trouble, not after the way he had left the big man hog-tied in Hy Loomis' cellar. Alone in the dark Jonas

166

hadn't tried to get away. He'd known the thing called law no longer controlled this man who'd pressed a gun into his back. McKee had sensed Jonas' fear. He'd read it in his blocky bandaged face while he'd tied him up. Jonas had watched McKee closely, never moving his eyes from Abrahamson's Colt or his own sixgun that McKee had taken from him.

They could break Jonas, McKee felt, once the threat of Basso's getting even with him was taken away.

McKee dropped all thought of Jonas as he passed through the deep shadow alongside his barn. His aim had been to get back to the yard and wait for Basso to come hunting. He hadn't planned on the crowd of men Basso had with him. He could see Royce, Cooley, Haycox, Tetterman ... and one of his neighbors across the street had come out onto his porch to watch.

McKee halted in his yard, all his hope draining out of him. There would be no careful wait out here, no chance to force Basso to fight on his own terms where the whole town could see the truth.

McKee heard the sound of knocking on his front door, then the talk which broke out among the men.

More knocking followed. More, louder talk. McKee drew the two sixguns from beneath his coat. They felt heavy and useless in his hands. He dropped them into the dark shadow thrown by the back steps.

The knocking banged again as he moved along his lawn. Sheriff Royce's voice carried clearly back to him, calling, 'Open up, McKee. Open up this door.'

CHAPTER SEVENTEEN

Cooley was the one who first saw McKee coming around the corner of the house. 'There he is, Mr Basso,' he announced. 'On the lawn.'

The men on the steps stared McKee's way. Cooley moved clear of the others and stood with his coat brushed back from his sixgun. The rest looked at Royce, waiting for the lawman to speak. In the moment of silence a window went up in a home across Main, and from the adjacent yard came the faint scuffing of shoes on sand.

'What's all that noise for?' McKee asked. 'I could hear you out in the barn.' To his left he noted that Ted Gilmartin and another one or two of his neighbors who'd been attracted by the loud knocking and talk were walking in close to hear.

Royce said, 'We want you to go up to the jail. We...'

'We're here for Jonas Foss,' Basso cut in. 'We can't find him and you were the last with him.'

168

'And you came here like this,' McKee said, looking at Cooley. McKee opened his coat so the men could see he wasn't armed. Cooley's body stiffened. He dropped his gunhand alongside his leg.

Basso said to the whiskered man, 'Go look in the barn, Cooley. See if he's got Jonas back there.'

McKee took a step closer to the cattle buyer. 'Please, Mr Basso, my wife's trying to get some sleep. She was hurt out at Walt Abrahamson's farm. The doctor gave her something to put her to sleep.'

'Hurt...' Basso repeated. He could not hide his surprise as he glanced at Cooley rounding the corner of the house. He recovered quickly and went on, 'I don't know what you're pulling, McKee. If your wife was hurt you can't blame Jonas.'

'I didn't say your bodyguard did it.'

Basso paid no attention to the remark. He motioned to Tetterman. 'I was told you were with Jonas, McKee.'

'That's right. I saw you,' Tetterman said. 'You went out of the saloon after Mr Foss. You crossed the street with him.' That brought low talk from the neighbors who watched. Basso's glance flicked from Tetterman to the people, and back to the long-faced hotelman. Tetterman, not so sure of himself, added, 'I didn't know your wife had been hurt.'

'She was shot,' McKee said. 'Do me a favor,

169

will you, Mr Tetterman? Get Doc Ward. He'll back up what I say.' McKee caught the louder conversation among the people. As Tetterman left, he spoke to Royce. 'You agreed with Haycox and Oursler that I wouldn't be bothered if I didn't go after Basso with a gun. You can see I'm not carrying one. I don't want all this noise around my house.'

'I shouldn't think he'd have to have it,' Ted Gilmartin said from the walk. 'Ben's got a right to keep things quiet.'

Royce said, 'Ben, you were with Jonas. All Mr Basso wants is to know where he went.'

'You take him in,' Haycox corrected the sheriff. 'After the trouble McKee has made, I think Mr Basso has a right to question him.'

'He can question me as much as he wants,' McKee said, his eyes on Basso. 'If I knew I wouldn't help him. The only thing I want is for you all to clear out so my wife can sleep.'

'Not until I see just what you're trying,' Basso snapped. 'You came after me with a gun. I think you'd go to any length to stop what I've attempted to do in this valley.' His gaze moved to Haycox, as if he expected the cattleman would add something. But Haycox was silent, his attention on Cooley who'd reappeared at the corner of the house.

Cooley stepped into the group. He said to Basso, 'I looked through the whole barn. Jonas isn't in there.'

A sudden troubled expression lined Basso's

170

face. It vanished as quickly as it had come. But the change was enough for McKee. He felt his quickened pulse-beat. He held his voice calm, talked directly to Royce. 'Sheriff, I'm asking you to move this crowd out of here. Charlotte...'

'I'm asking if I can look inside the house,' Basso said. 'I've got a right, Sheriff.'

'No, you have not.' McKee's voice hardened. 'You go into my home only if you have papers from a judge.'

'That's right,' a man called from the walk. 'I don't like all this, Nate. Beginning with that dog bein' poisoned when all our kids were there. Now this. Ben's got his rights, too.'

Other voices echoed that. More townspeople were joining the watchers all the time, serious-faced people who craned their necks to see and hear whatever went on.

'What do you say, Sheriff?' asked Basso. 'I want proof his wife was hurt. I think he's got Jonas Foss locked up in there.'

Royce wasn't looking at the cattle buyer. His mouth was tight, and his eyes were worried while he surveyed the spectators. Those close to the street had opened a path. Doctor Ward came up the walk. All talk ceased. In the dead quiet Basso absently rubbed his thumb and forefinger along the line of his jawbone.

The doctor halted near McKee. 'Ben, this noise isn't good for Charlotte.' Then, to Royce, 'Can't you hold this in your office,

171

Nate?'

'Ben said his wife was shot. How bad, Doc?'

'Seriously enough so she needs a great deal of rest and quiet. She's lost a lot of blood. She won't get the rest she needs with all this noise and excitement.'

Muttering went through the crowd. One or two at the street's edge broke off from the gathering and started towards their homes. A skinny old man in a faded blue suit and with a long, narrow, snub-nosed head, called above the talk, 'That's enough proof, Nate. I figure you should let Mrs McKee get her rest.'

Ted Gilmartin added, 'Ben, if you want, Rose will come over and give you a hand.'

'No, no thanks. Not yet, anyway,' McKee told him. 'In a couple days maybe, Ted.' He nodded to Royce. 'If Basso wants to go into this any further, I'm willing to talk it out in your office.'

'I think that's fair enough,' Royce said to Basso.

Basso's fingers rubbed vigorously along his jawbone. His voice pitched low, he snapped, 'I've talked enough.' His gaze bore into Haycox, then raked the watching faces. 'I'm not goin' to do any more talkin' in this town.' He started down the walk, with Cooley a step behind him.

The crowd fanned out toward the nearby homes. Nate Royce stood silent for a few moments, as if considering everything. 'I'll watch the house, Ben,' he said.

McKee shook his head. 'Don't, Nate. One way or another I've got to face Basso. It's got to be alone.'

Royce shifted his weight, glanced around at the departing townspeople. McKee thought the lawman was going to say something more. But, without a word, Royce turned, then moved along the walk.

McKee unlocked the front door and stepped inside his house.

Hy Loomis stood at the top of the staircase. He held the barrel of the Winchester aimed at the door.

'How's Charl?' McKee questioned.

'She slept through the whole thing. That must've been potent stuff Doc gave her.'

'Put out the lamp in our bedroom, Hy,' McKee said. 'Leave a light on in Maryann's room. You stay in the hall.' He took a step toward the kitchen, then halted. 'I left Jonas tied in your cellar. If this doesn't work out for me, you don't know a thing about it.'

Loomis nodded. 'You figure they'll come?'

'They'll come. You hear a noise you don't fight, Hy. Just start shooting so I know they're trying to get in by the front.'

'I will, Ben.'

McKee continued into and through the kitchen. He unlocked the back door as soundlessly as possible. After he was outside he locked the door again. He picked up the two

173

revolvers he'd left beside the stairs. Quickly, he crossed the moonlit yard to the open barn doorway. He stepped into the thick darkness of the first stall and stationed himself there to wait.

* * *

Giles Basso jerked open the hotel screen door. Behind him Haycox caught the door before it swung shut. He hurried into the lobby after the cattle buyer.

'I just want to know how soon we can expect your cowhands will come after our cattle,' said Haycox. 'If you could give me a date.'

'I can't give you anythin' right now.' He did not turn to look at the cattleman while he talked. He continued on past the registration desk and started up the staircase.

'I'll stay in town tonight, Mr Basso. I'll see you tomorrow.'

Basso did not answer him. He kept his back to Haycox, aware that the footsteps which followed him were Cooley's. Basso had his key in his hand when he reached his room. He jammed the key into the lock, turned it, and slammed the door in against the wall.

'Get the light,' Basso ordered Cooley. While the whiskered gunman struck a match, Basso stepped to the dresser and lifted the Greener shotgun. He had the double-barrelled weapon broken when the lamp flared and illuminated

174

the room. Basso pulled open a top drawer and took out a box of No. 10 shells. Two he shoved into the weapon. The remaining shells he stuffed into his right coat pocket.

Cooley stopped a foot behind Basso and picked a whiskey bottle and glass off the dresser's marble top. He tilted the bottle to pour the amber-colored liquid. 'Give these people time to settle down again,' he remarked, 'and I'll go start huntin' for Jonas.'

Basso whirled on his heels. One hand swung out and whacked the bottle from Cooley's hands. Glass shattered against the wall.

'Keep away from that stuff until this is finished. There's only one place McKee's got Jonas. Inside that house. That's the only place we look.'

Cooley's apple-cheeked face reddened under his beard and his hand fell to his side. 'Dammit, my workin' for you doesn't...'

'Shut up,' Basso flared. 'You shut up. I'm payin' you and that stupid Jonas five thousand each for this job, and you'll do what I tell you.' He had the shotgun's twin mouths pointed directly at Cooley's stomach. He waited and Cooley didn't speak. Basso moved his right hand away from the triggers. His fingers shook. He stared at them for a few moments, then grabbed the stock and threw the weapon onto the bed.

He cursed obscenely. 'That stupid oaf ... he must've found them and tried to get them by

175

himself. That stupid ... stupid...' He cursed again, looked at Cooley. 'Light the lamp in your room so anyone outside can see we're in here.'

Cooley opened the adjoining door and walked through. Basso moved to the bed. He picked up the shotgun, broke it, and checked the cartridges in the chamber. He closed the weapon. He rubbed his right hand against the shells in his pocket. He felt along the Colt underneath his coat.

Cooley reappeared in the doorway. 'Stay in there,' Basso told him. 'Go past the window every so often and let them see your shadow. Put your light out in ten minutes to make them think you're going to sleep. Soon as we're ready, you'll go get those horses Haycox let us take.'

'What 'bout that nosey clerk downstairs?'

'We'll wait 'til he's sleeping. If he stays awake, we'll quiet him before we go out, don't you worry.'

Cooley closed his door. Basso dropped the shotgun onto the bed. He walked close enough to the window to let his silhouette show on the shade while he slipped his arm from his coat. Then, when he had the coat off, he put out the wall lamp.

In the blackness of the room he moved a chair to the window. He raised the shade halfway and sat looking out. The dusty street was floodlight white under the almost full

176

moon, too bright to move right now. It was Sunday night and the business district was dark except for one light, the one inside the sheriff's office. That lamp was turned up high enough to throw its reflection into the street. The sheriff inside the office took no precautions to hide the fact that he'd placed his chair near the open doorway so he could watch the hotel.

Basso swore silently to himself and massaged his jawbone with his fingers. The satisfaction he'd felt when he'd first gotten to Buffalo Hole was gone. The fear he'd seen in McKee's face inside the store, McKee's disappointment when he'd been forced to give up his gun, the first bit of loss McKee had shown after the horse's leg was broken ... all were forgotten now. He'd have to finish things up fast and get away. The land and cattle company meant nothing. He'd built it up only for one thing. He could never go back to it once he started to run. But he'd still have all the money he'd put into accounts under other names.

Basso realized he was rubbing his jaw. He doubled his fist, tightening it until pain shot up along the tendons of his wrist.

He shivered and tightened the fist more. His body bent forward from the pain and he moaned deep in his throat. His face was close to the window now, and the moonlight caught in his eyes. They shone like a vicious wolf's.

CHAPTER EIGHTEEN

Sheriff Nate Royce was finding this long, drawn-out wait more unbearable each minute. He'd kept his vigil here in his office since he'd come from McKee's house. He'd waited with dread and eagerness, but nothing had happened. Basso's light had gone out almost an hour ago, Cooley's twelve minutes later. Royce had checked the exact time. He had been wrong all along about this trouble between Ben and Basso. His actions had only gotten him the contempt of the people. He'd heard the talk start after the dog was poisoned last night. He'd seen what it had grown to out there in front of McKee's. An armed law officer who'd failed to act when he should have—and every person in town knew why—deserved to be contemptuously ignored by everyone.

Royce got to his feet and paced his office, aware of the gunbelt's sagging weight around his hips. The heavy holstered Colt that dragged against his side might just as well be locked up in the rack ... He wasn't sure anything would happen. But he wanted it to. He needed this job so much, and the vote was out of Haycox's hands now. Emma was so sick. Billy and the baby would grow up here. They'd hear what would be said about their father. He paused by the corner of the door to peer out at the two darkened hotel windows. He couldn't tell a single thing that went on up there except that the lamps were out.

He looked up at the moon, lower toward the south, but still too bright for a man like Basso to chance being seen. It could be he was waiting for the moon to drop behind the western peaks.

A boot scuffed dirt at the right of the door. Royce turned with quick silence, his hand streaking to the anger and admiration. He grabbed the knife by the butt of the Colt. He was not surprised at his readiness, or the encouragement of the smooth-worn grip under his palm.

Ramon Lerrazza stepped up onto the walk. Royce backed away from the doorway to let the Mexican enter.

The dark-skinned man halted a foot inside the door. He stood stoop-shouldered and glanced across to the hotel. 'How does it look, Nathan?'

'I don't know. Ramon, I want the gun you've got in your pocket.'

'Ben McKee will need help.'

'He's got help, now.' The lawman made the statement quietly and slowly, certain of the answer.

'I told you, Nathan, after the leg of the horse was broken.'

'All right. I'm tryin' to make up for that. I don't want one town citizen breakin' a law for

179

any reason.'

The reproach made the Mexican's accent thicker. 'I could be sworn as a deputy. I am Ben McKee's friend. I want to help.'

The sheriff sighed. 'Give me the gun, Ramon. Go home.'

'I will help.'

'You won't help. Not by standin' here like this. Not if I let you stay here all night. Basso could be watchin' us right now. He sees the two of us waitin', he could put off what he intends to do. He could leave and come back some night in a few weeks when nobody could see him.'

For a long minute Lerrazza did not speak. Then his voice was clearer, weighed with reluctant acceptance. 'He will go after Ben.'

'I think he will. I watched him at Ben's house tonight. I believe he will' He held out his hand. 'The gun.'

Lerrazza drew a thick-handled Mexican knife from his pocket. 'I don't break any law, Sheriff. I will keep this.'

'You'll give it to me,' Royce exploded and, feeling the handle, took it from Lerrazza. 'You realize how close you'd have to be to use that. Go home, Ramon. Go home and stay inside. Please.'

'All right,' Lerrazza said placatingly. He turned and started across the street.

Nate Royce stepped onto the threshold and watched the tall Mexican until he'd vanished

180

into the shadows along the opposite walk.

Royce glanced up at the sky as if he was looking at the moon and stars, but his intent eyes searched the two middle hotel windows. He could not make out a movement behind the glass. There wouldn't be a movement, he knew now, as long as he let Basso see he was watching like this.

Royce backed into the office. He went to the cellblock door and closed it. He moved to the office's rear and unlocked the door to the yard. He blew out the lamp, took only a few moments to step outside and lock the office. Then he walked unhurriedly along the center of Main Street toward his home.

*   *   *

The last hour had passed very slowly for Ben McKee. The light in Maryann's room had gone out at nine, and since then the house had looked silent and dead.

He'd stood in just one spot all the time, not wanting to take a chance on making a single noise that could give him away. He tried not to think of anything but the house and yard, but he could not drive away his worry about the children. If Basso had somehow figured out what he'd done ... But Walt Abrahamson had his three sons with him, and they would keep a constant watch. He leaned against the corner of the stall and listened for one hint of noise.

181

He heard only the sounds of the warm summer night, the insect chorus and the far away drawn, rising wail of a coyote, breaking at the end in a shower of yelps that multiplied crazily along the stream bed. A horse nickered in a nearby barn, dogs barked now and then. Three houses away, the Royce baby woke up crying for a feeding.

The first close sound came from the right of the barn, a low scraping across the sand. McKee held the sixgun he'd taken from Jonas and cocked it while he moved to the doorway. His body flattened against the rough boards as he slid around the door, his gunhand raised for a shot.

A big white cat was at the rubbish box trying to force off the lid. The cat had heard McKee. It looked toward the barn, then scrambled away into the darkness. McKee's mouth was dry and his heart thumped. He took a deep, long breath, slid the Colt into his waistband.

He'd taken too long getting outside, he realized. He'd moved as quietly as possible, but the cat had still heard him. He'd have to find a better spot.

He turned and walked deeper into the thick blackness of the barn, past Queen's empty stall, to the ladder of the mow. He climbed up the rungs slowly, careful not to make even the slightest creak.

He opened the hay door in the front and sprawled out flat on his stomach.

He could see the entire yard and the lawn on the left side of the house almost to the street. The moon was lower to the southwest, throwing wide mountain shadows onto the grayish light of the valley. Where the land lifted in spots, sections of hayfields stood out like rocks emerging from water, silver and shining against the black velvet of the dip. Above, in the bluish night, the clear flakes of stars sparkled out endlessly beyond the moon. With a sigh, McKee dismissed the great silent beauty of the still landscape.

*   *   *

The moon dropped behind the peaks at four-thirty. The light faded while thick darkness rose up from the valley floor, the clearly etched houses and barns and outhouses taking on a fuzzy shading before the blackness engulfed them. The river breeze increased, became chillier. McKee placed the two revolvers on the boards beside him, buttoned his coat and turned up the collar. He strained his ears to listen, but he could hear nothing but his own slow steady breathing.

Somewhere in the black night, glass shattered.

McKee pushed himself up onto his hands and knees in the absolute darkness, his

183

reactions so numbed by cold and lack of sleep that it took him long and precious seconds to grope for his revolvers.

He held the solid hardwood butt of one weapon, Abrahamson's Colt, when the first shot came, the muffled and yet unmistakable sound of the Winchester, then the loud smashing of a window.

Forgetting the second sixgun, McKee crouched in the hay doorway and, bent almost doubled-over, he dropped straight to the ground. With both arms outstretched he broke his fall. He had his balance, was on his feet when more shots banged. One inside the house, two outside. Hy Loomis' loud wild yells tore out through Maryann's window. 'Watch them! Watch it! Two of them, one on the right side, other in front, breakin' in!'

A shotgun exploded around the front of the house. McKee, running hard, sobbed with fear and frustration, his thumping footsteps loud to him. He rounded the rear right corner and in that same instant a gun flashed halfway up the lawn.

He heard the report as the bullet jerked at his left arm, knocking him to the right away from the house. He felt no pain, only that the arm had suddenly become light-weight and warm. The gun ahead of him spat flame again. The slug zinged past on his left while he aimed at the spot where he'd caught the flash. He squeezed the trigger once, twice, raised the weapon an

184

inch in the final shot.

The man in front of him coughed, grunted, but the sound was lost in the second blast of the shotgun beyond the corner. McKee approached the man he'd shot and saw he was down. He slowed, holding the Colt's muzzle low. He didn't have to fire. Cooley lay on his back, wet sticky blood from the bullet hole in his forehead covering his cheek and beard.

McKee was moving again when the pain hit, tearing into his body from his arm like a white-hot knife. The breath left his lungs in a squeezing rush and he slammed himself against the side of the house to stay on his feet.

The Winchester cracked inside the building. Charlotte's scream quavered through the wall. Then followed a silence that was worse than the scream.

'Hy! Stay upstairs!' McKee screamed. 'Stay upstairs!' He half-fell, half-slid along the clapboards, reached the house's corner. 'Hy...'

The shotgun boomed near the front steps, smothering anything he could yell. The scattering blast of shot ripped onto the boards inches from McKee's head. He dropped to his knees, then sprawled flat, exposing only one side of his face while he aimed the Colt at the dark figure on the top step. He fired one bullet, a second, then the gun jammed.

Wildly, he pulled the Colt back in, grabbed at the drum with his left hand. His fingers

185

touched the cold steel, but they couldn't grip the drum to free it. McKee fought down the numbing pain. Nauseated, fearful, he whimpered, straining to force the hand to take hold.

He heard Basso's footsteps on the lawn, saw the shadowy form walking toward him. A noise came from Basso, a deep, guttural, snarling laugh unlike any human laugh McKee had ever heard before. 'McKee! You're finished, McKee!'

McKee dropped the left arm, straightened to his knees. He snapped the right wrist in a fierce final hope he'd somehow dislodge the Colt's drum. A lamp went on inside McKee's front room. Bright beams sliced down across the lawn, making Basso and everything within ten feet of him visible in the yellowish glare. There was blood on Basso's shirtfront, but there was no pain, no weakness, only hate in his confident, grinning face.

McKee heard a shout come from up the street, saw the dark figure of a running man in the same instant Basso looked around.

Basso paused, swung in a half-circle with the shotgun held level. The running man fired. McKee could hear the steel slug thump into Basso's body. Basso took a step toward the man, staggering.

Basso's shotgun blasted. The running figure was stopped in midstride, smashed back and down like a wind-felled tree.

Basso dropped the shotgun, then swung his shoulders around slowly, his hand reaching for his holstered sixgun. His lips moved as if he was going to say something to McKee, but his knees buckled before he could speak. He was dead when he struck the ground.

Hy Loomis appeared from the front doorway, the Winchester aimed and ready. McKee dropped the Colt and used his right arm to push his body erect. He stood and leaned his back against the house to get rid of the sick sense of floating he felt as he stared down at Basso.

More lamps had gone on. Lights were burning in almost every window around them, illuminating the entire area. The first few people who'd dared to come out now crossed Main. Others stepped outside, coats and robes over their nightclothes.

Loomis walked to the body in the street. McKee gripped the wounded arm with his right hand. He could feel the warm trickle of blood over his fingers.

Loomis walked stiffly, slowly toward McKee. He motioned behind him at the people who crowded around the body in the street.

'Nate Royce,' he said. He shook his head, grimaced. 'He took the whole load right in the chest and face. He must've been watchin' for this all night.'

McKee nodded. He tried to look at the dead sheriff, but the townspeople had crowded completely around the body. He could make out Haycox there, and Ramon Lerrazza standing in the rear of the crowd, crossing himself while his lips moved in a silent prayer. He stared down at Basso. The wide face had a strangely shocked look, and it was the color of dark-burned leather. The mouth was half-open, the white teeth shiny in the lamplight. Blood drenched Basso's white shirt in two spots, one an inch above the heart, the other in the center of the stomach.

'I put the lamp on so you could see,' Loomis said. 'He shot open the door, but he never got into the hall. He didn't get close to Charlotte.'

'Thanks. Thanks, Hy.' His tightened fingers had stopped the blood, and he was stronger. Reaction hadn't clouded any of his thoughts. The intense satisfaction he felt was dimmed only by the death of Nate Royce. He had no heart-pumping exhilaration within him, just a calm continuous realization that Charlotte and his children would no longer have to live in fear. They could live now, could laugh and pick up their lives ... He took a slow step along the side of the house, then hesitated.

'Hy. Will you take Ramon and Haycox up to your house to get Jonas?' He gazed at the people. Most remained around Royce, but a few were already crossing the lawn to look at Basso. 'And tell Haycox I want to see him back here as soon as you have Jonas locked up.'

'I'll tell him, Ben.'

The front door hung on its top hinge. The bottom had been ripped loose when Basso's shotgun blasts had splintered the entire bottom half wide open.

Inside the house Charlotte waited at the top of the stairs. She had her blue bathrobe on over her nightgown. Her face was drawn and white, and she stared fearfully at McKee's bloody arm.

'Oh, Dear Lord,' she whispered. 'I thought you were all right when I heard Hy talking to you.'

'I am all right, darling. We're all all right.'

'Yes,' she said slowly. She seemed to pull herself together, took a step toward him. 'Come into the bedroom. Hy will get the doctor.'

He nodded. He intended to put his arm around her and let her help him, but a sudden weakness made him lean against the wall. He sat down on the top step.

She sat beside him, and he leaned against her. They could hear the people talking out on the lawn, but they could not make out the words clearly enough to understand anything. Somehow it didn't seem important.

'I've got to go over to Royce's as soon as I can,' he said. 'I'm taking Haycox in with me. I want Emma and Billy to know the whole story.'

Charlotte nodded her head. She didn't speak, for Doctor Ward had stepped into the hallway. The doctor started up the stairs. McKee squeezed his wife's hand. 'We'll get some sleep after,' he said quietly. 'Then I'll drive out and bring the kids back home.'